"So, you like dominant women, do you?" Grace asked.

"Oh, yeah," Ben groaned, as she moved on top of him.

Taking a wild guess at what else he'd like, Grace clamped her thighs together and pushed her hips forward, holding his arousal hostage to her whims. Ben's breath caught and Grace discovered she was enjoying having Ben where she wanted him.

"I can play the same game you can," she said raggedly, hoping she wasn't lying. "I can tease and torment as long as you can, probably longer. And I will. Until I know why you've been fighting the attraction between us."

"You don't want much, do you?" *Just his soul,* Ben thought. Her damp heat surrounded him and she'd begun a steady clenching of her pelvic muscles that nearly sent him over the edge.

Her warm brown eyes met his. "I want you, Ben."

And as much as he knew he shouldn't do this, *couldn't* do this, Ben wanted her, too. And looking at their intimate proximity, it wasn't as if he was in a position to argue. "I'm all yours, Princess."

Dear Reader,

Seduction. How many of us dream of being brazen enough to go after the person we desire, no holds barred? Grace Montgomery not only has those dreams— she makes them come true! She is stepping out of her shell and discovering her sensual side, thanks to her sexy new neighbor, Ben Callahan. The chemistry between them sizzles and when Grace decides to seduce him, Ben doesn't stand a chance! After all, he's the first man who appreciates Grace as a woman instead of a wealthy socialite. She can't help but fall in love with him. Trouble is, Ben isn't the man Grace thinks he is...

Speaking of dreams, writing for Harlequin Temptation BLAZE has been a fantasy come true for me. I'm constantly in awe of the talented company I now keep. And thanks to Harlequin, my dreams will continue, bigger and better than before. Look for Harlequin's newest—and hottest—series yet, Harlequin Blaze, to launch mid-2001!

I hope I'm making your reading fantasies come true. Write to me at P.O. Box 483, Purchase, NY 10577. Or check out my Web site at www.carlyphillips.com.

Happy reading,

Carly Phillips

Books by Carly Phillips

HARLEQUIN TEMPTATION
736—BRAZEN
775—SIMPLY SINFUL
779—SIMPLY SCANDALOUS

SIMPLY SENSUAL
Carly Phillips

Carly Phillips
2001

TORONTO • NEW YORK • LONDON
AMSTERDAM • PARIS • SYDNEY • HAMBURG
STOCKHOLM • ATHENS • TOKYO • MILAN • MADRID
PRAGUE • WARSAW • BUDAPEST • AUCKLAND

To friends, old and new. You know how to listen, how to care and I know I can count on you when things get rough. For Kathy Attalla, who has always been there, and for Janelle Denison and Julie Elizabeth Leto, who fate luckily brought into my life. This one's for you!

And to my editor—Brenda Chin—for always believing in me, even when I don't believe in myself, and for having the good taste to let me write Grace's story and revisit Emma Montgomery, one of my favorite characters...
Thank you!

ISBN 0-373-25915-8

SIMPLY SENSUAL

Copyright © 2001 by Karen Drogin.

Visit us at www.eHarlequin.com

Printed in U.S.A.

1

BEN CALLAHAN FROWNED at the bone china cup on the sterling serving tray in front of him. Unable to fit one of his large fingers through the handle, he tried instead to hold the delicate cup with his whole hand. He'd have chucked the idea of attempting to grasp the cup, if not for his elderly hostess. Emma Montgomery had declared it was teatime, and from what Ben had seen, he wouldn't be getting any information out of her until he'd shared in her daily ritual.

He'd never understand the wealthy, nor did he care to try. He'd had a good deal of experience with the breed, none of it leaving a positive impression. His mother had scrubbed floors for a living and he'd seen firsthand how poorly the help was treated. He'd whisked his mother away from menial labor and verbal abuse as soon as he was old enough to support them both.

It was ironic, really. Most of the clients he'd accumulated as a private investigator had money to burn. Ben didn't mind taking their cash. It paid not only his bills, but the extra money covered the cost of the independent living community where he'd placed his mother. He considered it payback for her years of service.

The elderly woman seated across from him was a potential client. She'd been referred to him by an acquaintance in her social set, one he remembered from the time he'd worked for her last year. So far Emma Montgomery, his hostess, had been refreshing, both charming and persistent at the same time.

While other clients tried to whittle away at his expenses and final take, despite their ability to afford his reasonable fee, Emma Montgomery had paid his airfare and expenses from New York City to Hampshire, Massachusetts, to discuss her reasons for wanting to hire him. As further enticement, she'd named a hefty sum he'd never seen before on a single case, and promised him free rein with expenses, no questions asked. All *before* she'd explained why she needed his services.

Ben was not only intrigued, but inclined to accept. The money she'd promised would enable him to have his mother moved from independent living to assisted care. With her eyesight rapidly deteriorating, she couldn't live alone and this case might make the upgraded care possible. If it meant putting up with idiosyncrasies like teatime, he'd force himself to endure.

He met his hostess's gaze. Piercing brown eyes regarded him from over the rim of her cup. *I'm waiting,* she seemed to be saying. There was nothing he could do but raise the cup and take a sip.

The minute the hot liquid passed his lips, she said, "My granddaughter needs a sitter. Do you have any interest in the job?"

He swallowed fast, burning his tongue and nearly losing his precarious hold on the fine china. No way he'd heard her correctly. She was offering all that good money for him to play baby-sitter? He shook his head. "Excuse me?"

"Perhaps I didn't phrase that quite right. I think maybe keeper is the correct word." She tapped the side of her head, without messing the perfect bun in her gray hair. "Yes, that's right. My granddaughter is in the process of finding herself and she needs a keeper."

He placed the cup onto the saucer before he could do serious damage. "I think you've been misinformed, Mrs. Montgomery." Good money or not, Ben drew the line at baby-sitting.

"Call me Emma." Her smile grew wider.

"Emma. I'm a private investigator. I don't baby-sit wayward children. Just how old is your granddaughter anyway?"

Emma reached onto the table beside the couch, holding a photo in her hand. She turned the picture toward him.

The woman staring back at him was no child. Honey-blond hair, warm brown eyes and a face as delicate as the china he'd recently held stared back at him. A rush of desire hit Ben hard and a shot of adrenaline jump-started his heart.

"She's almost thirty and quite a beauty, isn't she?" Emma asked, pride lilting her voice.

He met the older woman's gaze and shifted uncomfortably in his chair. "She's...something all right." A golden princess.

In his profession Ben was used to observing people and photographs. He was used to forming opinions and going with gut instinct. He was rarely mistaken in his impressions and never blindsided by a pretty face. And he'd always been able to remain detached. Until now.

This woman was beautiful enough to affect his senses and sensual enough to rev up his libido. Her eyes reflected a wealth of emotion and hidden secrets—secrets he yearned to uncover. The assignment he'd been about to throw away had suddenly become one he couldn't resist and a distinct sense of unease slithered through him.

"Grace moved to New York City a few years ago," Emma said. "She's always lived off the trust her parents set up for her as a child. No steady job, no steady man." She said the last with enforced meaning before she appraised Ben from his work boots to his unkempt hair.

He shook his head as if he could rid himself of her penetrating stare. "And what's going on with Grace that's prompted you to contact me now?"

"She's stopped withdrawing money from her trust and decided it's time to live on her own."

"I'd think that was an admirable move," Ben said,

having more respect for the new Grace than the one who had lived off her family money for years.

"Well, of course it is. It's how I raised her, after all— To be her own person. It worked, to an extent. She got out of Hampshire and away from her controlling father, Edgar, who is my son. We call him the judge." She laughed but the sound contained no joy. "He has no idea what family means. Though I admit, with my grandson, Logan's, recent marriage and new baby, he's learning. But Grace isn't around to see it."

Sensing she'd gotten off track, Ben tried to steer her back to what she wanted from him. "So you want Grace back home?"

Emma shook her head. "Not if she's safe and happy in New York. That's all I care about, you see. But I can't get information out of her because she's clammed up on me." The older woman zipped her fingers across her lips. "All she'll say is that she's fine and I shouldn't worry." Emma snorted, telling Ben what she thought of her granddaughter's silence. "How can I not worry, the way she travels with a camera around her neck, paying more attention to her photographs than her surroundings?"

"She's an adult," Ben felt compelled to remind Emma.

"Women like her are attacked every day in New York City. She swears she's taken a self-defense class, as if that's enough to soothe me. I'm certain she's holding out. Ever since my brush with death, she thinks she's protecting me. She doesn't realize it's more stressful on the heart, being kept in the dark."

Ben nodded in understanding. His own father had died of a heart attack when Ben had been eight. He remembered him as a good man with a heart of gold. Too bad that heart had also been weak and he'd died driving home from his job as a department store manager, leaving no insurance and little money in the bank. His mother had been forced to extreme measures to make ends meet, and she'd turned to the only experience she had—housekeeping, only this time she worked in other people's homes.

"Make no mistake, Mr. Callahan. I'm glad Grace is finally ready to tackle the world on her own." Emma's voice brought him back to the present. "It'll give her a chance to sow those wild oats her father made her suppress, but at the same time, that kind of sudden freedom frightens me. Even nearing thirty Grace has been sheltered too long. And I know her. Now that she's made a stand, her pride won't let her call on me or her brother if she runs into trouble. I need to know she's okay." Emma placed a frail hand on his arm.

"Call me Ben," he said, wondering if Emma was right—if Grace had a penchant for getting into trouble, and if so, what kind.

No way he could deny Emma the peace of mind she sought. Her obvious love for her granddaughter, along with his financial need, sealed his agreement.

She smiled. "I've taken a few liberties under the assumption you'd take this case."

Ben was used to presumptuous clients, but he could only imagine what this woman had decided for him. "What liberties would those be, Mrs...." He caught the quick shake of her head and corrected the formality. "What liberties, Emma?"

"Grace lives in Murray Hill, in a one-bedroom off Third Avenue. After a long talk with the landlord, I managed to secure you the apartment across the hall. It seems his brother lives there and he's out of the country on business for the next month." Her white smile widened. "Wouldn't it be nice of his good friend Ben Callahan to apartment-sit for him?" She reached for something on the sofa table behind her and dangled a set of keys in front of his eyes.

Ben shook his head. "How convenient." He thought he'd been prepared for anything. He'd been wrong. "I'm sure you realize I already have a place to live, Emma."

She rolled her eyes as if he were slow. "Of course you do." Without warning, the older woman grabbed for his hand again, and her eyes met his in a silent plea, one he had a hard time ignoring. His gut clenched as he silently acknowledged he was in trouble.

"I need to know Grace is safe, satisfied and fulfilled before I pass on. And you can only do that if you get close enough to see for yourself. I've heard you're the best, Ben."

He knew he was being worked shamelessly, and even so, he couldn't look away. Worse, her motives seemed so honest and pure, he couldn't bring himself to turn her down. What would it hurt if he got to know the granddaughter to assure the grandmother everything was okay? He could give the older woman peace of mind and finance his mother's care at the same time. A win-win situation, even if it meant putting up with the older woman's meddling.

"Well?" Emma asked.

He glanced at the photo once more. Detachment? Hell, he'd been sucker-punched by a picture. Heaven only knew what his reaction would be to Grace Montgomery in the flesh.

Emma patted his knee. "That's okay. All men react like that the first time they see her."

Was that supposed to make him feel better?

"I suppose you realize now why she needs someone to look out for her, especially since she's on her own and more vulnerable than before."

Ben had his doubts Grace was as naive as Emma painted her. After all, she'd been living in the city and even with money to burn, she'd have learned to be cautious and careful. Still, he understood and felt the older woman's concern.

Ben let out a groan. With little effort, he'd become invested in both Emma and her granddaughter. More than he should be with a client. Enough to warn him away from this case.

He stared into those compelling brown eyes and

knew he couldn't walk away. Emma's obvious love and concern for Grace was one reason, his financial needs another. But there was yet another, more elemental reason not to opt out, his personal misgivings be damned. If he bailed, Emma would find another private investigator to get up close and personal with her granddaughter.

At a glance, Ben knew he couldn't trust himself around Grace. But he sure as hell wasn't about to let someone else take the job, either.

ADRENALINE PUMPED THROUGH Grace's system, a natural reaction to the afternoon spent capturing pictures that filled her soul. Unlike her temporary job at a photo studio specializing in portrait shots, her time at the park held the key to her future and she reveled in every minute. Even a routine stop at the corner grocery store hadn't dulled the sense of excitement she found doing what she loved, and if her instincts were on target, she'd captured exactly the right shots.

She juggled the bags filled with necessities while attempting to pull the apartment key out of her poncho pocket. There was so much flowing material she could barely find the opening. She understood now why the tailor had balked against sewing a pocket into the cape, but she hadn't wanted to give up the garment in favor of her more sensible denim jacket. Given to her by her beloved grandmother, the poncho had once allowed her to hide her camera from the rest of the family who hadn't understood her artistic obsession any more than they'd understood her.

She had escaped to another state and a huge city to be on her own, experience life and discover the real Grace Montgomery. Her likes, her whims, her future. Ironically the move alone hadn't accomplished her goal. She'd ended up living off her trust, continuing to emulate her family because, subconsciously, she'd sought the approval she would never receive. It had taken her brother, Logan, and his recent wedding to the most real, down-to-earth woman Grace had ever met to shake Grace up and make her realize she wanted what Logan had: a life of her own choosing.

Once again, irony played a role. Though Grace had divorced herself from the snooty country club set back home, she'd kept in touch with her closest friends. Cara Hill, a woman Grace both liked and respected worked tirelessly for CHANCES, a charity that benefited underprivileged children. She was putting together a brochure and had purchased a huge layout in a high-circulation magazine aimed at enlightening the wealthy about the problems faced by people outside their social circle.

Raising substantial cash was the goal and Cara was taking a chance on an unknown photographer—on Grace—to capture that real world and the children who inhabited it. Grace refused to disappoint her. The experience could lead to more jobs and ultimately a photography career that paid the bills and left her fulfilled at the end of the day.

She felt the cold, metal key between her fingers at the same time the first brown bag toppled out of her arms and crashed to the floor. She glanced down at the white plastic bag and groaned. "It would have to be the eggs."

"Another dinner party shot to hell?" A lazy masculine drawl sounded from behind her.

Instinct told her the sexy voice belonged to her new neighbor. Instinct and the curling warmth in her belly. She closed her eyes and held the feeling close. It matched the one she felt whenever she caught a glimpse of him out her window. The first time he'd been unloading a black Mustang packed tight with clothing and accessories. Her neighbor, Paul Biggs, an investment banker, was away on business and the super had mentioned she'd be having a new neighbor living across the hall.

He'd turned out to be a sexy new neighbor, in tight jeans and a faded blue T-shirt that clung to an incredibly sculpted body. Grace came from a world where men were soft and manicured. A specimen like him was just one of the treats of living far from home, and she'd enjoyed watching him from a distance.

Steeling herself for their first meeting, she set the rest of the bags on the floor. She turned, and although she'd glimpsed him through her window before and even snapped a few photos with her camera, she discovered nothing compared to seeing him in the flesh.

He stood across from her, one shoulder propped against the chipped wall. Once white, the dingy paint now held a gray tinge, and still her neighbor's jet-black hair stood out in stark contrast. Tousled from an apparent jaunt outdoors, his dark hair reached his shoulders and begged for a woman's touch.

Her touch. She swallowed hard and wondered where *that* notion had come from? She'd never been tempted to stroke a man's hair before but nothing about him was like anything she'd ever encountered. He oozed raw sexiness and called to something primal and elemental inside her. Something she hadn't known existed—until now.

He was pure male testosterone in a package that said, "Don't mess with me." And she was suddenly struck with how much fun it could be to do just that.

"Looks like you could use a hand. I'm Ben Callahan, your new neighbor." His voice brought her out of her musings.

She realized she'd been staring and extended her hand. "Grace Montgomery."

"I meant a *helping* hand." He laughed, a seductive rumble that set her already raw nerve endings on fire.

Before embarrassment at her too-formal behavior could take over, he stepped forward and placed his large, warm palm inside hers. "It's nice to meet you, too."

Heat arced between them, sizzling and hot. Ben cleared his throat, then quickly released her hand, leaving Grace to wonder if he was as unsettled by the sensations as she.

He quickly composed himself and she wished she could do the same.

"Can I help you with those packages?"

She shook her head. "No, thank you. I can handle them." But she couldn't handle him or her reaction to him as easily.

"Well, my mother taught me never to let a lady struggle, and besides," he said with a slow grin, "I like helping beautiful women." Without waiting for her response, he stepped around the groceries, bent down and collected her bags.

She turned toward the door, key in hand. Aware of his heat and strength behind her, she put the key into the lock and let them into her apartment.

"Where to?" he asked.

"Just put them on the kitchen counter." She pointed to the small pass-through that led to her working kitchen.

He deposited the bags, broken eggs included, onto the butcher-block countertop and turned. "So was I right? Did you ruin another dinner party by dropping the groceries?"

Obviously he was referring to last night's parade of women who'd come to her apartment. Once Grace realized her job for CHANCES also enabled her to capture fabulous candid shots of children, she'd begun making copies—and the parents came by once a week for coffee and free photos. Considering her privileged upbringing—that she hadn't worked for or deserved—it was the least she could do.

Although Grace hadn't realized Ben was monitoring the comings and goings from her place, as an expression of his interest, it would do nicely.

She shook her head. "No dinner party, now or then. Nothing more planned than an evening in front of the TV. And last night wasn't as big a bash as you seem to think."

"I thought I might have missed out on a good party." Curiosity lit his features as he met and held her gaze.

Warmth trickled through her veins. "Nope. Just a few friends over. Would it soothe your ego if I said your invitation got lost in the mail?" She grinned, unable to help the smile he inspired.

He laughed. "No, but it would help if you threw a welcome-to-the-building party in my honor."

"I...uh, think that could be arranged." Her boldness surprised her.

As much as she enjoyed their easy banter, this meeting had thrown her badly. She inhaled deeply. His musky scent seduced and aroused—and would now linger in her apartment long after he was gone. Her life, which just yesterday had been filled with routine and concern about making it on her own, now had spark and zing. Inspiration, she thought, glancing at the man in the fitted T-shirt.

He was everything that intrigued her in the opposite sex, nothing like the kind of men who'd asked her out back home—the suit-and-tie, suck-up to Judge Montgomery type of man, who had turned her ice-cold. And though she'd been just another anonymous female in New York City, she hadn't given much thought to dating since her move. Not after the last couple of setups courtesy of her friends had turned into boring disasters.

Nothing about Ben was boring. She took in his rugged good looks, his sexy, bad-boy posture and attitude. There wasn't a thing about him, from his alluring scent to his heated touch, she didn't enjoy. Why not make use of her discovery?

Professionally Grace had already begun the starting steps toward a life of her own. On a more personal level, she'd become so used to turning down dates in favor of her own company, her femininity and wiles were rusty from disuse. But thanks to Ben Callahan that was about to change.

Whether he knew it or not, he had just become the second step on her road to self-knowledge.

She leaned toward him, a whisper away from temptation. "So what did you have in mind?"

A lazy smile lifted one side of his mouth and caused her to realize she'd backed herself into a corner. A very attractive corner.

"I'd like to get to know you, Grace."

She smiled. "Sounds good to me." She liked his boldness. She'd had her fill of too polite men who wined and dined but weren't honest about their intentions. Ben let her know up-front who he was and what he wanted.

He'd implied he was available. Though Grace

wanted to be bold and daring, all *this* was too new. She wasn't ready to reveal that she desired to get to know him, too, but she had every intention of satisfying his request.

His aura of confidence appealed to the part of her that wanted to feel the same, and time with this man could teach her a lesson or two in self-esteem. He brought out a newer, bolder side of herself she wanted to experience again. Not to mention that the man was a feast for the senses and a boon to her sensual awakening. The knowledge set her heart jumping and myriad intimate possibilities raced through her mind. Her breath caught in a noticeable hitch.

She licked her dry lips and watched, fascinated, as his eyes followed the movement. Without warning, his gaze darted from hers and he turned away.

His sudden retreat was unexpected and hard to understand, but she let out a slow exhale of relief. The reprieve would give her a chance to catch her breath.

Hands in his back pockets and posture erect, no indication of interest or flirting in sight, he walked past her and glanced around her small apartment. "One bedroom?"

"Yes."

His hand swept over the living area, replete with Oriental rugs and porcelain decorative pieces. "Beautiful place."

"Thanks." She'd decorated the apartment in the days when she'd still been living off her trust, before she'd figured out how to realize her dreams or even what they were. Though she wanted this man to see more to Grace than the trappings of wealth, she wasn't about to get into explanations now, not when she knew so little about him.

She turned back to her kitchen. "I really should unpack the groceries."

"Grace?"

She glanced his way.

"Something wrong?" he asked.

Other than the fact that his hot-cold act confused her? But if his feelings were rampaging as quickly as hers, she could begin to understand. "Nothing's wrong. Just lost in thought. It was nice meeting you, Ben."

"Likewise." He hesitated, then reached out and stroked a hand down her cheek. Another sudden change toward her. His fingertip lingered, his touch a sizzling combination of heat and electricity.

His eyes widened and he withdrew once more, confusion and regret sparking his gaze, leaving her to wonder again if he was as thrown by their first meeting as she.

"See you around, Gracie."

She inclined her head. "Bye."

He walked out of her apartment with a sexy stride she couldn't help but admire. The door slammed shut behind him and Grace hugged her arms tight around her chest, amazed at the feelings and sensations he inspired.

Ben brought out the side of her she'd suppressed

while trying to live by her father's rigid rules. The only time she'd snuck out of the house to meet friends at a local bar, she'd lived to regret it. Her father had embarrassed her badly. He'd called every parent, gotten her friends grounded for weeks, and no one had spoken to Grace for an equally long time.

The judge had accomplished his goal. She'd never rebelled again. But in her sexy neighbor Grace saw the opportunity to do just that with no painful consequences.

When she'd decided to branch out on her own, she'd desired change in her life. She hadn't known it would come in the form of her sexy, intriguing neighbor, Ben Callahan.

But she intended to take full advantage.

2

I'D LIKE TO GET TO KNOW YOU, Grace.

Ben smacked his hand against the wall. What the hell had he been thinking, speaking with his gut and not his brain? He'd spent the past five days watching her from a distance, yet he'd underestimated the impact she'd have on him upon meeting her in person. He'd meant to be friendly and begin to gain her trust.

Instead he'd been blown away. Her cocoa-brown eyes had danced with light and life and he'd been captivated on the spot. Adrenaline had kicked in the second he'd heard her soft voice, and surrounded by her fragrant scent of vanilla, his body had come alive. He'd backed off, but not soon enough. Even a cold shower hadn't lessened the effect of Grace Montgomery.

Small consolation but at least he'd made substantial progress on the assignment, and in less than a week's time. When Emma called for her daily report—in about five minutes, he noted, glancing at his watch—he'd be able to tell her he'd met her granddaughter.

Ben paced the floor of the apartment. No need for the older woman to know he'd been enchanted and completely caught off guard. The picture hadn't done Grace justice and Ben knew for certain if he wasn't careful, he'd fall hard and fast for Emma Montgomery's free-spirited granddaughter—a woman far out of his league and the subject of his investigation to boot.

Perhaps because of his father's careless ways, Ben's work ethic was strong. He worked hard, provided for his mother, saved for the future when he could, and made certain his clients were happy enough with his services to secure a referral for future cases. His work ethic did not include playing around with a client's granddaughter.

He had to focus on his job and, in fact, he'd made quite a bit of headway. He had Grace's routine down pat. Not only did he know she had a full-time job at a photography studio uptown, but he knew she spent her lunch hour and weekends frequenting a park that bordered a seedy neighborhood.

Ben knew all about neighborhoods where trouble lurked. He'd grown up in one and knew just how tempting a woman like Grace could be to a guy from the wrong side of the tracks. Hell, he knew how she tempted him now.

He had no problem putting Emma at ease about how Grace was earning money to survive, but he'd hold off before revealing the rest. Ben needed to do some more digging into other areas of Grace's life to find out why she was hanging around questionable parts of town, camera in hand. The faster he got the information, the faster he could get the hell out...before his rapidly beating heart was broken by a woman who'd undoubtedly grow bored with her new life.

She might be living on her own, and he admired the attempt, but sooner or later, Grace Montgomery would miss the family she'd left behind and desire the easier lifestyle she'd grown up with. The expensive decor of her apartment proved she hadn't completely left the life behind.

Ben didn't begrudge her that life. He just had no intention of being a casualty when the novelty of making it on her own wore off.

GRACE STEPPED OUT of the dark subway station. The freedom she felt walking into the fresh air, camera in hand, the breeze warm on her arms and the sun hot on her face, was liberating. She passed by the boarded-up building that once held a restaurant, waved to a bunch of neighborhood kids she saw on her daily trips to the park and rounded the corner leading to the playground she loved.

As usual during lunch hour, the basketball courts were crowded with kids and she paused in front of the wrought-iron gate. Clutching the cold metal in her hands, she peered through the open spaces and watched the games from the sidelines. The smack of the ball against the blacktop mingled with the low strains of male voices. With most of the players in white T-shirts, Grace was hard-pressed to tell them apart...until she caught sight of the guy in gray.

She couldn't mistake the jet-black hair hitting his shoulders as he ran or the physique she'd memorized the day he'd moved in. But it was the distinctive sound of his voice over the dull roar of the other players that sealed her certainty. She didn't know what Ben Callahan was doing down here, and she intended to find out. But not until she'd captured this moment on film.

She hadn't seen him for a week and she had no intention of letting the opportunity to feast on his good looks and masculinity pass her by. She flipped off the lens cap and raised the camera to eye level. At the same moment, play on the court stopped, the guys hitting the benches to take a break—except for Ben and a lone player who remained by the hoop. Though Grace stood in the shade of the buildings' shadows, Ben stood bracketed by sunlight.

Her week of deprivation was at an end and she paused to revel in the sight.

He wiped a hand over his forehead to remove the sweat and grime from the game—a typically masculine move, but there was nothing typical about Ben. His sexy mannerisms, his powerful stance, the muscles in his legs visible thanks to his nylon shorts, set him apart from the other men in the world. And Grace appreciated it all as she began to capture his movements on film.

His body language mimicked those around them.

He spoke to the kids as if he knew their language, as if he were accepted. Yet she'd never seen him here before. Grace wondered who he was and why he'd shown up now. Did he know the neighborhood residents because he worked in the area or did he have family down here? she wondered.

But first...with the easy adjustment of her zoom lens, she zeroed in. With each click of the shutter, she became one with Ben, and as she seized his every nuance, every undercurrent on film, she began to *feel*. Her heart raced as if she'd run the court and her pulse pounded in time to the dribble of the ball smacking the ground.

As he gestured and moved, explaining something to the youth beside him, she couldn't draw her gaze from the ripple of muscle in his arms and the strength in his calves and thighs. Thanks to the sun's strong rays and his hard play, damp stains darkened his T-shirt. She snapped the shutter automatically, not missing a beat, but her body continued a rampage of its own. Her back grew damp and her shirt stuck to her skin, while a fine sheen of perspiration dotted her face. She lowered the camera and inhaled deep, drawing an unsteady breath.

Grace had been searching for clues to what kind of woman lay inside the polite female created by her judge father and well-bred mother. Now she knew seething sensuality lay dormant inside her, just waiting to be unleashed. And Ben was the man to take her on the next part of her journey of self-discovery.

Everything he made her feel was honest and real, so opposite to the artificial world she'd grown up in—a world where people hid their feelings, married for show, cared little for their children, and worst of all repressed their sexuality—unless they were cheating on a spouse. Except for her brother Logan, who'd defied the family political tradition and had also married for love, the Montgomery world was a phony one.

The opposite of the real world Ben inhabited.

She could only imagine the strength and beauty of the photos she'd just taken—photos for her personal album, not a stepping stone in her career.

Another glance at the court, and she saw Ben once more, hand on the kid's shoulder, apparently explaining the finer points of the game. Not many men cared enough to work with the kids in this neighborhood, kids who needed guidance. Grace admired not just Ben's physique but the obvious goodness he possessed inside.

She headed around the gate and came up behind him. "Hey there, neighbor."

"Grace?" He turned toward her, surprise in his voice, disbelief in his gaze.

"The one and only." She sprinted onto the court to join him.

He tossed the ball to the young boy. "Get to work on those jump shots. I'll be with you in a second." He pivoted back to her. "What are you doing here?"

Was that anger she heard in his tone? She raised an

eyebrow in question. "Well, hello to you, too. And I could ask you the same thing. It just so happens I'm a regular around here. How about you?"

"What's with the camera?" he asked without bothering to answer her question.

She lifted her prized piece of equipment before letting it fall back around her neck. "I'm working. What's your excuse? Because if you don't mind my saying so, it seems awfully coincidental that we'd both end up in the same neighborhood."

He met her gaze, which was a good sign that he wasn't hiding anything, but she didn't know him well enough to read him...yet.

"Don't get yourself worked up, Gracie." His voice softened and she couldn't help melting like ice cream on the hot sidewalk. "I was just concerned to find you hanging in a neighborhood like this." His arm swept the air around him.

She figured that was as much of an apology as she would get from the man. "Well, I admit it's not as fine as most, but the people here are real." Considering concern was behind his attitude, she didn't mind explaining. "And they deserve the same little joys in life the rest of us have."

She waved the camera. "That's what these pictures are for, to help raise money on behalf of the kids in this neighborhood—and the mothers love them. Pictures of their kids are the least I can give back." She silently cursed the insecurity she hadn't meant to reveal.

He stepped forward. "And why is that?" His soft voice wrapped around her like a warm caress. "Is your background more privileged than most?"

"How'd you guess?" she asked, suddenly wary. Because they'd met once and she'd never revealed her background to her neighbor. Of course her apartment decor reeked of wealth, but his tone held more than a hint of certainty that he knew her well.

He lifted her chin with his hand, holding her face up to daylight. Heat having nothing to do with the sun skittered across her skin. "That cultured voice is a dead giveaway. And besides those sculpted cheekbones speak for themselves."

So he'd pegged her from day one. But to Ben, she didn't want to be the spoiled rich girl, she wanted to be just Grace. And she believed she still had that chance.

She inhaled deep. The air held Ben's raw scent and if Grace thought she'd been swept away by the sight of him before, she was on fire now. "What makes you such a good judge of people?"

"In my line of work, being observant is second nature."

She shot him a questioning look.

"Private investigator," he explained.

His occupation surprised her, but she appreciated the insight. "Is that what you're doing down here? Working on a case?"

She glanced over her shoulder, hoping the kid Ben had been coaching wasn't the subject of some undercover investigation that would get him in trouble. Drugs, the illegal sale of fake merchandise—she saw too many kids in danger and hoped the money from CHANCES would help kids like these. Not only would it open the door to her career, but she'd ease the guilt she felt for having so much when others had so little.

"Now, Grace, are you avoiding the question about your background?" He not-so-subtly turned the subject back to her.

She grinned. Apparently, with their interest in each other running high, neither one was willing to give without receiving in return. "No, Mr. Private Investigator. Let's just say I'm leveling the playing field. You answer my question, I'll answer yours."

He fingered the camera strap between his thumb and forefinger. "I didn't know this was a game, but I'll play. Since I'm new to the building, I asked the landlord which areas to avoid and he mentioned this neighborhood. High crime, drug trafficking...kids in need." He pointed to the game of basketball that had resumed behind them. "So here I am."

She'd found this neighborhood in much the same way, but she was a permanent resident. Ben was a temporary neighbor, which made his actions that much more generous and giving.

She wondered again what was behind his presence here. "Why, Ben, I'd never have suspected you had an altruistic streak."

He laughed. "I don't go around advertising it, but I

grew up in a place like this. Whenever I go in to a new neighborhood, I like to go back to my roots. Like you, I give back in return."

Her chest constricted at the admission. So not only was the man of her dreams sexy, but he had a heart.

"No welching. It's your turn. *Is* your background more privileged than most? Is that why you feel the need to hit these areas without backup?"

She laughed. "I don't think I need backup. Who'd be interested enough to bother with me?"

"Don't underestimate your worth, Grace."

She shivered, realizing he'd struck her one weakness with deadly accuracy. Though she hadn't meant to imply she wasn't worthy of interest, it was her greatest fear. That her worth lay only in her money and family name.

"I meant who'd give me a second look? I'm dressed in rags." She pointed to her ripped jeans and paint-splattered T-shirt. "No makeup, no jewelry to attract attention." She shrugged, hoping she'd covered any hint of insecurity she might have revealed.

"Just a fancy camera worth good money in a pawn shop, for starters. Then there's those cheekbones I mentioned earlier." His finger slipped down her face, whisper-soft but with enough electricity to light this neighborhood in a blackout.

"I can take care of myself."

"I know you believe that, but..."

"I *know* that." She grasped his finger in her hand. The desire to feel the rough glide of his skin over her aching breasts was overwhelming. Somehow she found the ability to speak. "I appreciate the concern but I really need to get going. I want to shoot a few pictures before I have to get back to work."

He stepped backward and the distance gave her breathing room. "You owe me some answers, Gracie."

She laughed, grateful to be off the hook for now. "That's okay. I'm not going far."

Before he could answer, she turned and headed for the playground. Little did Ben know, she wasn't kidding.

He was the key to her sensual self-discovery and she planned to get very close to him, very soon.

BEN SHOOK HIS HEAD, watching as her behind swayed gracefully in tight denim. Her name suited her perfectly, Ben thought. Which was why *Grace* had no business being in this neighborhood.

Hell, he didn't like being back in an exact replica of his old stomping grounds. With little money growing up, the basketball courts had been his escape. The harder he'd pounded the ball, the more he'd thought he would forget that he'd be coming home to an empty apartment. No father, a mother who was working too hard, and neighbors screaming at each other on both sides of the paper-thin walls.

He related to the kids he'd met this morning when he'd stationed himself here to wait for Grace. If Ben could get one in particular, Leon, to keep his focus on the game and not the streets, the kid could get a scholarship and make his way out of the slums. Ben's time here would be well spent, not to mention that helping the guys was a distraction from Grace—who still hadn't given him a strong enough reason for hanging out in a place like this. He admired her desire to give back. He respected her for the effort. But he'd hate to see her good deeds rewarded by trouble.

And why did he care? Ben let out a groan. This was exactly what he didn't want—to get involved in her life. His job was to find the facts for his client. Instead he was thinking about Grace too much, words like admiration and respect coming to mind as he did.

No sense in denying the truth. Far from the detachment he'd promised himself, he was beginning to care. Being around Grace could put his heart at risk and he didn't like it worth a damn.

Better he focus on the facts of the case—he'd gotten the answers Emma had sought, in record time. He knew Grace's professional occupation and how she filled her free time. He could see for himself she was indeed happy as Emma wanted for her granddaughter. If her choice in locations wasn't prime, well, she was a smart woman and an adult—she could take care of herself.

Distance, he reminded himself and turned back to the court. Leon threw him the ball, catching him off guard. Ben began a steady dribble, echoing the word detachment each time the ball smacked the blacktop. He went for a layup at the same moment a feminine, familiar shriek pierced the air, sounding over the raucous voices of the guys in the game.

His gut clenched hard. Ball forgotten, he ran toward the sound of Grace's voice. She was sprawled on the ground where she'd obviously been pushed, and a tall kid in a red sleeveless, hooded sweatshirt pulled on the camera strap around her neck. His strength nearly lifted her off the ground, while Grace, looking petite and out of her league, refused to hand over her precious possession.

"Hey!" At the sound of Ben's shout, the youth released the strap, causing Grace to fall backward against the pavement. Given a choice between running after the attacker or seeing to the victim, Ben chose Grace.

He knelt down beside her. "You okay?" Long strands of blond hair fell over her face and he brushed them aside with one hand. Ignoring the sensation of silk beneath his fingertips wasn't easy.

She offered him a smile he had no doubt was forced. "I'm fine as long as you don't say 'I told you so.'"

"I don't have to. You already did." He held out a hand to help her up.

She placed her palm inside his, wincing as her skin slid against his coarser flesh. Grabbing her wrist, he gently turned her hand over to reveal angry red scrapes on her palm. "Other one?"

She flipped over her right hand. Similar abrasions

covered her skin. "It's nothing some antiseptic won't take care of."

"Agreed." But his insides didn't feel as calm as his voice. A queasy feeling settled in his stomach at the sight of the bruises, and an uneasiness pricked at him when he thought of what could have happened if he hadn't been around to scare off her attacker.

She swiped at her eyes. So she wasn't as brave as she wanted him to believe. Good. In that case he wouldn't have to worry about her returning here when he was gone. He pushed aside the added grief that thought caused in his gut.

He helped her rise to her feet without putting pressure on her hands. "You weren't going to hand over the camera, were you?"

"Of course not! That camera cost a bundle. I couldn't afford to replace it and, besides, he's not entitled to take what doesn't belong to him."

He laughed at the innocent proclamation along with the determined clench of her jaw. "And just how did you plan to stop him?"

"If he'd gotten the camera, I'd have tripped him before he got two feet away. But you saved me the hassle. And besides, I held on to the camera, didn't I?"

The little minx sounded proud of herself.

"He could have snapped your neck."

"But he didn't. See?" She whipped a fall of blond hair off one shoulder, exposing delicate white skin.

But Ben wasn't fooled and he pulled back on the camera strap, cringing as he saw the damage. "Your neck doesn't look much better than your hands, Gracie. Ever think of taking a self-defense class?"

"I haven't had a chance, but I'll make time—soon."

Obviously she'd lied to her grandmother about having taken those classes. What else had she lied to Emma about and what else was she doing in this neighborhood?

"Thanks for the help, Ben." Her shoulders slumped and much of the earlier bravado went with it as a tremor shook her slender frame. Taking him off guard, she turned and walked away.

"Hey."

"Is for horses," she called over her shoulder.

Two long strides and he caught up with her. Though he admired her independent streak, he was too worried about her to leave her alone. Hell, he *wanted* to be with her after what had just happened. Though he was asking for trouble, taking care of Grace came first.

Shoving his hands into his pockets, he walked alongside her. He sensed her need to keep moving, to not think about being attacked. She was probably in shock and he understood. But the numbness would wear off and he planned to be there when the impact set in.

"Where are you off to?" he asked.

"Subway."

He shook his head. No way he'd let her go alone. The first few times he'd followed her, he'd ducked into a crowded subway car and tailed her at a discreet

distance. Today, wanting things to appear coincidental, he'd taken his car.

"Subway's not safe."

She stopped in her tracks and turned toward him.
Glazed but determined eyes looked up at him. "It's
been safe enough for as long as I've been coming
here."

"So was the neighborhood until today. Let me
drive you home. My car is around the corner."

Gratitude flickered in her eyes, but she shook her
head. "No, thanks. I can get home myself."

"I'm sure you can." Unable to help himself, he
reached out and touched her cheek and she turned
her face into his open palm, until he cradled her face
in his hand.

She was so soft. Her skin, her voice...but not what
was inside. Emma knew her granddaughter well.
Grace was tough. And as much as she might want to
give in, she wouldn't let herself lean on him.

He admired her strength, even if right now, he
wanted to conquer it. "There's nothing wrong with
accepting help every once in a while."

She smiled. "I know that."

"Then lean on me now." He treated her to his most
charming grin. "And I promise I'll let you ditch me
later." And he hoped to hell she did toss him out. Because Ben wasn't sure he had what it would take to
drag himself away from her.

3

GRACE HANDED BEN the keys and let him unlock the door to her apartment. She was too tired to do it herself and, besides, her hands stung worse than when she'd fallen off her bike as a kid. She wasn't ready to think through today's ordeal—or the threat the punk had made to her before Ben ran him off.

Stay out of this neighborhood, or else.

She squared her shoulders. Just because he'd scared her to death didn't mean she'd listen to threats. Grace came from a family of strong people who did what they wanted, the rest of the world be damned. And though she rarely cited her family as having virtues, this time, she was prepared to emulate that one trait. After she took care of her cuts and bruises and after she got rid of Ben. His strong presence made it too easy to want to lean on him. Too easy to succumb and lose the thread of independence she'd begun to weave.

He stepped inside and held the door open for her to do the same. She walked past him. He wasn't dressed for the office, his hair was mussed and hadn't seen a barber's scissors in quite a while. Still, he was the most appealing sight she'd ever laid eyes on.

Independence be damned, the man was right. Leaning on him wouldn't be so bad. In fact she'd probably enjoy it and heaven knew being around Ben made the threat of danger seem less real.

"You can put the keys and camera on the shelf." She pointed to the etched glass shelf "floating" from the wall.

He stepped around her. The keys made an unnaturally loud sound as they clattered onto the glass. "You need to take care of those hands."

She nodded.

"Where's the antiseptic?" he asked.

Someone else taking care of her was a novel experience, which was probably what made it so appealing. Except for her grandmother, no one in her family ever made her feel loved for herself. Her mother tried, but thanks to her father's bullying, she'd always fallen short. But for her brother, Logan, no male in her family had ever made her feel warm or cared for. In fact, her father, with his impossibly high standards and demands, diminished her self-worth and made her more insecure than any child ought to be.

But Ben had held her the entire walk to his car, making her feel safe and cherished. After seeing him with the kids at the park and viewing his unwavering concern for her now, she knew more than sexual attraction drew her to him.

She tipped her head upward and met his concerned gaze. He caused her to feel a whole host of emotions. None platonic. All solid and good.

"Grace? The antiseptic."

She gave herself a shake. "In the kitchen. The cabinet to the left of the microwave." She followed him the short distance and waited in her small walk-in kitchen while he sorted through the cabinet and came up with a light antiseptic to clean her cuts, an antibiotic cream and bandages.

He took the box off the shelf and held it up for inspection. "Barney?"

Grace felt a heated flush creep up her face. "I knew I ought to keep something in the house just in case, and well...that's all they had."

He laughed, his features softening, a dimple appearing in his right cheek. She raised her hand and touched a finger to the enticing crease. His skin was hot and rough with razor stubble.

He sucked in a startled breath and she dropped her hand. "Don't play with fire, Gracie. Unless you want..."

"To get burned?" She met his heavy-lidded gaze. "I admit to liking the idea. I always had to be the good girl. I never crossed the street without an adult and I never played with matches. I'm tired of being good. I *want* to play with fire." She wanted to play with him.

Though she'd never been so bold before, something about Ben made her feel free...to be herself, Grace realized. And it felt good.

His hands came to rest on her hips. Large palms and hot skin.

Before she realized his intent, he lifted her up and placed her on the kitchen counter. "First we see to your hands and neck."

Grace smiled. Let him tend to her injuries first. She'd get a chance to question him more about who he was and where he'd come from. The pull between them wasn't going anywhere anytime soon.

"Turn your hands palms up." Ben desperately needed the distraction of caring for her injuries before he forgot them in favor of her enticing yet innocent proposition.

She did as he asked. He washed his hands at the sink, then returned to her side and saturated a cotton ball. With care he wiped down her dirt-streaked hands, cleaning the scrapes. Except for the first time when she sucked in a pain-filled breath, she didn't utter a word of complaint and let him work.

"You're good at this. Get much practice?"

He recognized her attempt to distract herself from what must sting like the devil, but he also recognized a feminine ploy to extract information.

Still she was so guileless in her attempt, he couldn't help but indulge her. "No younger siblings to take care of if that's what you're asking." He reached for a fresh piece of cotton to pat down her hand and then opened the antibiotic cream.

Using his thumbs, he gently rubbed the center of her palms, massaging the ointment into her pale but soft skin—skin marred only by the bruises inflicted when she'd hit the sidewalk. The urge to lift her hand to his lips and ease her pain was strong.

The urge to comfort warred with the more primal desire to wrap her in his arms and protect her from harm. And it had nothing to do with the case.

Damn, but Grace Montgomery was trouble.

"How about children?" she asked.

At the blunt, out-of-the-blue question, his finger pressed against her hand too hard and she let out a gasp. "Sorry. Jeez, Grace, if you want to know something, just come out and ask." He glanced up at her sheepish expression.

An embarrassed but endearing smile worked its way onto her lips. "You caught me, I guess."

He laughed. "Let's just say your investigating skills need some brushing up."

She shrugged. "Good thing you're just the man to teach me." She paused. "Unless there's a wife, child or girlfriend I don't know about?" Curiosity and hope mingled in her warm brown eyes.

"No wife and child, no girlfriend and no exes with kids, either. But I meant brushing up on more discreet ways of getting information." He peeled open the ridiculous-looking bandages with the purple dinosaur and patched her hands as best he could. "I'll make a drugstore run later and pick up something better to cover those hands, at least until they're feeling better."

She glanced down at his handiwork. "You don't

need to make a special trip. I can live with Barney until tomorrow."

He ignored her protest. If a drugstore trip was the only way he could escape he'd take it in a heartbeat. He ignored the devilish voice in his head reminding him of what other items could be found at a drugstore should the need arise, and he refocused on her injuries. "Okay, now for your neck."

She winced at the thought of him repeating the procedure on the burn left by the heavy camera strap rubbing against her skin.

"I think we can forget the antiseptic and just go with the cream."

She exhaled a sigh of relief. "Sounds good."

"Let's see."

As she brushed long strands of hair off the side of her neck, she made room for him to take a look—by spreading her legs and letting him step inside. Surrounded by her feminine heat and intoxicating scent, Ben realized he was in trouble.

Fingertips covered with ointment, he touched her neck as gently as possible. A tremor shook her body, and her thighs clamped shut, enclosing him in her warmth. An echoing shudder overtook him.

He had to clear his throat in order to speak and, even then, his voice came out a hoarse whisper. "Can we skip the bandages, too?"

She turned her head and her face was a tempting millimeter from his, her lips within kissing distance. His mind demanded he walk away. His body refused to listen to reason. He opened his mouth to speak, to prevent the inevitable, when she took advantage of his indecision and touched her lips to his.

Hot. Sweet. Demanding. Giving. The swirl of emotions flowed inside him as urgently as her tongue swept inside his mouth. Her hands gripped his forearms, heedless of the scrapes on her palms, and her nails dug into his skin.

Good judgment be damned, Ben thought and answered her silent plea, sealing his lips over hers. She moaned and he swallowed the sound, threading his fingers into her hair. The strands felt like fine silk beneath his fingertips, a stark contrast to the hardness building inside him.

A shred of sanity remained—the part of him that knew he ought to stop now, before things went any further. He grabbed her wrist, calling for her attention.

She tilted her head back. Eyes glazed with desire, she met and held his gaze—until the ringing of the telephone shocked him back into reality.

He tried to push back, but Grace's legs held him tight. "Let the machine get it." Her soft stare never left his and her labored breathing matched the beat of his heart.

Three short rings later he heard Grace's husky voice directing callers to leave a message, followed by a beep and a too-familiar voice.

One guaranteed to instill guilt. "Hello, Grace. It's been too long since I've heard your voice. I want to know how you're getting along in the big, lonely city. Met anyone interesting lately? You know I wouldn't mind a great-grandchild from *you* before I pass on. And if that's too much to ask, how about a little information about your life instead? After all, the woman who raised you ought to..." A beep cut Emma's voice off, indicating the older woman had run out of time.

But not wind. Ben had a hunch she'd still be rambling if the machine hadn't taken care of the problem. Somehow he managed to stifle a combination laugh at Emma and self-directed groan. He wasn't supposed to know Grace's grandmother—any more than he was supposed to be kissing Grace.

The grip on his waist loosened and he took advantage. He stepped back into the safety zone, out from between her legs and out of her reach.

She gestured toward the telephone. "I'm sorry." Her voice didn't sound much steadier than he felt at the moment. "Emma, my grandmother, has impeccable timing, even long distance."

"She sounds like quite a character."

"Oh, she is. But a lovable one, and she worries about me."

"What was it she started to say? She raised you?"

Grace nodded. "She was the only adult in the house who cared about me and my brother—about how we felt, not how we appeared to the outside world. I adore her." Warmth and kindness softened her voice.

Her relationship with Emma seemed to parallel

Ben and his mother's and he could understand her strong feelings for the woman who'd raised and cared for her. "Then I'd say you were lucky to have her around."

Grace laughed wryly. "You can't possibly feel that way now."

Considering Emma had placed him firmly back in reality, reminding him of his job and what his relationship with Grace was supposed to be, Ben most definitely appreciated her call.

"But she has good reason to worry, wouldn't you say?" He turned the conversation back to Emma's message.

Grace's gaze darted from his. "Until today, not really," she said, lightly.

Her soft laugh didn't fool him. This afternoon's attack had shaken her up more than she was willing to admit. Why else had she sought to release her adrenaline with that heart-stopping kiss?

"Why don't you just stop by every once in a while and reassure her?" Ben asked, to keep conversation flowing. But he hated lying to her, even by implication.

"She lives in Boston."

"Ah. You're a New Englander. That explains the accent."

"Hampshire, Massachusetts, born and raised. But I really don't want to talk about me."

He raised an eyebrow. "Then what would you like to talk about? And don't say that kiss because it never should have happened." No matter how great it was, he silently added. Women tended to dislike being told they were a mistake. But for Ben, being honest with Grace was the only way to avoid finding himself in this predicament again.

"Oh, really?" She folded her arms across her chest. "Care to tell me why not?" Unfortunately she didn't seem the least bit upset about his comment.

"I took advantage of your injuries."

A smile curved her lips. "I'd say I took advantage of you. But instead of quibbling, why don't I just tell you what I want to talk about?"

Without waiting for a response, she jumped right in. "I want to talk about you." Using her hands to brace herself, she hopped off the counter, then winced.

"You okay?"

She nodded. "I just have to remember to watch myself for the next few days."

"At least you have the weekend. Unless you have someplace you have to be, like work?"

"I work at a portrait studio uptown, but I'm off Saturday and they're closed Sunday...which reminds me. I need to call and let them know why I never showed up after lunch."

"Go ahead." He gestured to the phone. While she made her call, a wave of relief washed over him. He wouldn't have to follow her around and watch her back for the next two days because she'd take care of herself at home. He'd have a reprieve.

"The owner was very understanding." She hung up the receiver. "I'll rest up today but I'm working on a freelance project in my spare time, so I can't afford to sit around and pamper myself because of a few scratches."

He was curious about the project she'd mentioned but more concerned about her safety. He narrowed his gaze. "You're not planning on heading back to the park, are you?"

Her shoulders stiffened and she lifted her chin a determined notch. Not a good indication that he'd get his wish on this. And definitely not a sign she was pleased with his interference, either.

She let out a slow exhale. "Any reason why I shouldn't go back there?"

"Other than the obvious?" Much as he'd love to back off and respect her independence, he couldn't.

"No punk kid is going to run me off. I come from stronger stock than that and I don't respond to threats."

"Threats? *Threats?* What haven't you told me, Grace?"

She opened her mouth to speak, then shut it again, clamping her jaw tight. Apparently she'd decided not to let him in on whatever he'd missed back at the park. If she thought keeping secrets would deter him, she was wrong.

"Grace?"

She bit down on her lower lip. The same lip he'd kissed, and sucked into his mouth minutes earlier. He stifled a groan and concentrated on what was important: her safety.

She shook her head. "You're doing it again, you know. Changing the subject."

"If you ask me, you're doing the same thing."

She grinned. "But we're talking about you." She stepped closer. "And you're avoiding the fact that I had a question of my own. I want to know about you."

He shook his head in exasperation. Emma was right. Grace needed a keeper. Like it or not, he'd have to stick close at least until he knew more about the threats she'd mentioned, and until he discovered what was behind today's attack. Suddenly it didn't seem as random as he'd originally thought.

He spread his palms wide and played along, treating her to an easy grin. "Ask away. I'm an open book."

"Good. Then you won't mind telling me how long you're staying across the hall?"

He lifted her chin and looked into those brown eyes. "I wouldn't mind at all, if I didn't think you had an ulterior motive. What's up, Gracie?"

She stepped closer, until he could inhale her scent and practically taste her glistening lips. "I just want to know how long I have to seduce you."

SEDUCE HIM. Grace had uttered those words with such complete certainty that even twenty-four hours later Ben was still aroused. The hell of it was, he didn't think he could deny her if faced with an all-out assault. One he felt certain would come. Grace now knew she had three weeks to act—or not act, if he had his way.

After her proclamation, he'd answered her question and made a quick exit. She should have taken the hint. But her soft laughter had followed behind him, telling him she didn't consider his hasty retreat a defeat. Considering the feelings rioting inside him, she had every reason to feel victorious.

If it were just her sexuality he had to deal with, Ben felt certain he could easily maintain his professional distance. Instead he found himself faced with a beautiful woman he also respected and admired. Walking away from her trust fund when it would have been easier to give in and live easy, spending her days at the park to give back to society—he'd yet to discover what that meant, but he sensed great import behind her words. She was generous, caring and gutsy. And though he'd withdrawn last night, he didn't know if he'd have the strength to do it again.

What Grace didn't know or understand were the reasons for that withdrawal. So far she hadn't asked. But she would. And he couldn't give the simplest explanation without revealing he was being paid to investigate her and he wouldn't betray a client's trust without permission. Emma's trust had to come before his personal feelings, never mind the money he'd see from this case.

But he never wanted to face Grace's wrath should

she ever discover he'd deceived her. He felt guilty
enough as it was and guilt was an emotion alien to
him when dealing with the subject of an investigation—another clear sign Ben was in too deep.

He hooked a hose up to the building's outside
spigot and dragged it over to his car. The high-rise
boasted not only a doorman, but a circular driveway
with plenty of room to spare. The super, being a car
fanatic himself, hadn't minded Ben's request to hand-
wash his old Mustang outside the building. He
needed the distraction even more than his car needed
cleaning.

He squeezed the sprayer on the hose and began
watering down his car. As he bent for the bucket of
soapy water, an uncomfortable sensation of being
watched pricked at him. He shook off the feeling,
knowing he was surrounded by high-rise apartment
buildings and windows galore.

Impossible, Ben thought. But the longer he stayed
there, the stronger the feeling grew.

4

GRACE LOWERED THE CAMERA and placed it down on her dresser. A light sheen of perspiration tickled the back of her neck and blood was pumping fast and furious through her system—a result of both watching Ben and worrying about the day to come. She stretched, arching her back and feeling her sore muscles from yesterday's struggle with her attacker. She shivered at the reminder and decided some raw courage was in order.

She couldn't live in fear of walking through New York City, nor could she avoid the neighborhood where she'd made friends and had found a source of perfect photographs for the CHANCES brochure. She had to get back on the horse, so to speak. But she'd do it the first time without the camera. She needed to face down her trouble, not look for more. And she needed to go alone.

By the time she headed outside, Ben had soaped his car into a good lather. She could slip by him with a quick wave and there was nothing he could do about it. But she took one look at him and all her intentions dissolved in a puddle of soapy water.

He'd stripped off his shirt and her first glimpse was

of his bare back. Muscles in his upper arms and shoulders rippled each time he wiped down the car with a soft rag. She couldn't walk away from him any more than she wanted to.

He was a mystery beneath the tough-guy exterior. A private investigator, he'd said. An intriguing profession for an intriguing man, a man she admired for going back to low-income areas similar to where he'd grown up. It took guts to return to your roots—Grace ought to know, considering she'd run from hers.

She stepped up behind him. "Working hard?"

He turned, one arm propped against the side-view mirror. "I'd hardly call this working. I'm just grateful to have the day off."

"I know what you mean." The sun beckoned overhead, already warming her arms and legs. Though she could go to the park on her day off, she could also afford to follow his lead and take a few hours to herself first.

"Where are you off to?" He glanced down at her sneakers and narrowed his gaze.

She could read his thoughts and knew he was worried she was heading to the park alone. She appreciated his concern but didn't want the argument. Besides, she'd already decided to hold off on her jaunt.

She held up her hands in mock surrender. "Nowhere you have to worry about." Yet, she thought.

She walked around the car, sliding her hand over the cool metal as she inspected the gleaming exterior. "Good job. Have you started on the inside?"

He shook his head. "Not yet."

She rolled up the sleeves on the jersey she'd swiped from her brother's drawer before he went away to college. "Then let me help."

"What about your hands?" He reached out to take a look. His hot touch singed her skin and she felt the pull inside her as well.

"Barney's got them covered."

He still held on to her hand. She didn't know if he was even aware of it, but she was. And along with the enticing sensations he inspired, a wave of determination rose in her chest. She'd spent her childhood suppressing her desires in favor of the good-girl role. She'd finally broken free and, thanks to Ben, she had the chance to experience being bad.

With her window of opportunity limited to three weeks, she had every reason to be more brazen and bold, no matter how difficult the act. She drew a deep breath and rubbed her thumb over his more callused flesh.

He jerked his hand back in surprise, then turned toward the car. "Go ahead and help. If you're sure you're up to it..."

"I am."

He gestured to the pile of supplies on the ground. "Then get to work."

She bent, picked up a dry rag and a bottle of spray cleaner and climbed into the front seat. Though she'd left the door open, sitting in Ben's small car, she was enveloped in his scent, in the essence of what made him sexy and real. Chemistry, a subject she'd never understood but now appreciated, was at work. And as usual, when it had to do with Ben, it made Grace burn.

She wondered as she wiped down the inside of the front window what would make a man like Ben lose that rigid control. She darted a glance out the window and, to her amusement, she caught him watching her before he jerked his attention back to whatever task he'd been doing. It wasn't the first time she'd caught him looking, and after a few minutes passed, she realized it wasn't the last.

She slid out of the car and leaned against the exterior. "It's hot out here. It may only be spring, but it has to be near seventy already."

"Perfect day for a car wash," he said from his position on the opposite side, where he was working on polishing the hubcaps.

"Yup. A girl can work up a good sweat if she's not careful." Gathering her courage, she lifted the hem on her jersey and pulled the center upward, tucking the bottom into the rounded collar and yanking down on it. The result was a bikinilike top. A shirt that had once covered too much, now covered very little.

"Whew." Grace made a show of fanning herself with her hand. "That's better."

Her voice captured his attention and he walked around to her side of the car and took in her outfit. He looked her up and down thoroughly—just as she'd hoped. Then he flipped his sunglasses off and hung them on an empty belt loop.

"For a better look?" she asked with a grin.

A muscle worked in his jaw, and if Grace had to bet, that rigid control of his was hanging by a delicate thread. He exhaled hard. "Get back to work before the landlord revokes my washing privileges," he muttered.

Mission accomplished, she thought and let out a sigh of relief. This being naughty was not only fun, but she wasn't too bad at it, either.

Grace saluted and climbed back into the car. "I haven't had the chance to do anything like this in a while," she called out to him. "When my brother turned sixteen, he got his first car. A brand-new..." She clamped her mouth shut. She'd spoken without thinking and swallowed a curse, wishing she could choke on the words to avoid revealing the truth.

Why was it all the little facts of her childhood she'd taken for granted before embarrassed her now that Ben had come into her life? Even when she'd decided to forego her trust fund, she hadn't been quite as ashamed of her background. She shook her head. Well, shame was a good thing. It would teach her humility and help her appreciate all the things she now worked to achieve.

He paused, obviously picking up on the silence. "Brand-new what?"

"Porsche," she said under her breath.

He let out a slow whistle. "Nice."

She cringed and held on to the futile hope he'd change the subject.

"And what did the princess get when she turned sixteen?" he asked.

So much for hoping. She crinkled her nose and glanced up at him. "The *princess?*" She hoped he caught the disdain for the term in her voice. She wanted him to appreciate her as a down-to-earth woman.

He braced his arm on the roof and leaned into the car. "You. Princess Grace."

His face was so close she had the desire to reach out and touch the razor stubble on his cheeks. To play with the fire he aroused. But she suddenly wanted more between them than pure sexual attraction.

She wanted him to both like and respect her, the way she liked and respected him. She might not know much about him, but his character spoke volumes. He was a knight in shining armor, helping the underprivileged and caring for damsels in distress. She stifled a laugh, knowing he wouldn't enjoy her description.

She didn't want to be the unattainable princess in the locked tower. "Is that how you see me?"

Ben caught the disappointment in her tone and felt like a heel for using an obviously sensitive subject to his advantage. He didn't understand why her background always sent her running for cover, not when she was making an independent stand now.

"Princess," he murmured, repeating the word,

softer this time. "Is calling you that such a bad thing?"

She raised her hand to touch his cheek. "If it puts me out of your reach it is."

But that's where he needed to be—out of her reach. So he'd used the term princess, on purpose. Considering her brazen assault, he'd figured he could be forgiven for treading on touchy ground. Now that he saw the vulnerability in her eyes, he wasn't so sure the ends justified the means.

"I meant it in the nicest possible way." The excuse sounded pathetic even to his ears.

She snorted in disbelief. "Yeah, right. Okay, this isn't the first time you've asked or alluded, so I'll tell you all about my background, okay? I come from a wealthy New England family, just like you thought. An uptight, staid, don't embarrass us or betray your roots kind of clan. We've got political tradition dating back to the early 1900s and not one divorce in our history. Want to know why?"

He heard the bitterness in her tone and regretted opening this can of worms. He hated having caused her the least bit of pain.

"Why?" he asked, partly because she expected him to, but mostly because she so obviously wanted to get this out in the open between them.

"Because Montgomerys don't divorce, they endure." Her features contorted in disgust at what sounded like the family motto. "For the last five or six generations, the Montgomerys did what was expected. They married the so-called *right* people. The result was miserable unions, infidelities, unhappy children they ignored—none of it mattered as long as outside perception was good." She shook her head in dismay.

Ben didn't attempt to stop the explanation he knew hurt her badly.

"My brother, Logan, was the first to break the mold and I'm proud of him. Not for betraying his heritage but because he's happy. Me? I'm working on it. But in the meantime, yes, I've learned the art of perfection in public and maybe that's where that princess image you have of me comes in. It's so deeply ingrained I don't even realize how I'm behaving half the time." Her shoulders dropped in relief. As if by revealing, she'd released a huge burden.

Ben didn't kid himself. Just because Logan had broken free didn't mean Grace would be able to do the same. That public perfection she'd mentioned was apparent in the way she carried herself, although less so in the way she acted. And damn but it was just one of the things that drew him to her. Amazing that the world he disdained had shaped the woman he desired.

She was a woman with shadows lurking in her eyes right now. He wanted to take her in his arms and protect her from the memories he'd evoked. Because it would only complicate things, he refrained.

"There's more," she said.

He shook his head. "I appreciate the honesty, but you don't have to do this."

Her gaze met his. "Yes, I do. You need to know one last thing. All that money I mentioned doesn't do a bit of good if you're unhappy or you lose yourself in the process." She shrugged and her cheeks turned pink, as if she was embarrassed by the admission.

He'd known the facts from Emma, yet hearing Grace's view of her world, he could almost believe she'd walked away for good. Almost. He knew she meant every word she'd uttered. But once she found herself and everything she was looking for, going back to the money and the life she'd left behind wouldn't be as difficult as she thought. As she'd said, it was second nature.

But right now, that world was far away. And what he saw in front of him was a vulnerable woman. One who'd gotten to a heart Ben would have sworn wasn't capable of deep emotion. Before Grace, he'd never *felt* so much before.

And that was yet another reason to back off. He reached out and grabbed her hand, holding it briefly. For reassurance. For selfish need. "We'd better get back to work."

She let out a slow breath, but was obviously relieved the subject was closed for now. "Anyone ever tell you you're a slave driver?"

He laughed but it sounded harsh to his own ears. "I can think of worse things to be." Like a liar, he thought in disgust, wondering when in the hell doing his job had become something that turned his stomach.

For the next hour, they worked side by side. Rather, she worked and he admired... He admired her attention to detail, her diligence at scrubbing coffee stains off the dashboard, and the way her behind moved in tight denim as she scrambled to her knees and wiped down the center console.

He shook his head. He had no doubt every move was calculated to capture his attention. Damned if he wasn't mesmerized anyway.

"Time to call it a day." She climbed out of the car, looking wrinkled, messed and every inch *not* the Grace Kelly image he'd tried to paint her in. She was as beautiful, regal and striking as the young Princess of Monaco had been, but at this moment, she was also dirt-streaked and rumpled.

His Grace wasn't a princess. She was real. Enough to make him forget her background and his case—if he was looking for trouble. He told himself he wasn't.

But his throbbing body didn't agree. And neither did the part of his brain that both liked and admired Grace Montgomery.

She wiped her hands on the front of her jeans, drawing his attention to the pull of material at the fly. He tried to swallow but his mouth had grown dry.

"I'm through here. Take a look and take a whiff. The fresh scent of clean." With a bow, she waved, meaning to give him a look at the inside of his car.

What he got was a glimpse down her makeshift

shirt instead. Two rounded mounds of white flesh swelled over delicate lace. He shook his head to distract himself, then bent and peered inside the car, hoping to get sidetracked. His old seats shone and the scent of lemon-lime surrounded him, but his mind was firmly on Grace.

He straightened and met her gaze. "Good job, Gracie."

"Really? Thanks." The flash of white teeth told him she was proud of her handiwork and even more pleased by his compliment.

"How long has it been since someone told you you've done good?" He was suddenly certain her discomfort with her background was related to her occasional bouts of insecurity.

"Too long. Especially from someone I...care about." Her cheeks grew pink at the admission.

So his instincts had been right on. Ben had no doubt Emma bolstered her granddaughter's self-esteem as much as she could, but nothing could replace parental pride. From all the insinuations, Grace's father's parenting tactics could use some work. Ben had been fortunate with his parental luck of the draw, both his mother and father had supported him emotionally and had always shown their love. But Grace apparently hadn't been as lucky.

He looked into her beautiful face and was glad he'd been able to contribute something positive to her life after all. Even if she didn't realize it, he did.

"I really have to be going," she said.

He reached for her but she stepped back. "Where to?" As if he didn't know.

"The park. And playground. The sun's out and to-morrow's forecast says rain." She backed up another step.

"Okay. Give me ten minutes to clean up and I'll go with you."

"No." She shook her head. "Absolutely not." She stepped backward again. "I need to do this alone. And I know you understand that—respect it, even. If you can just put those caveman instincts aside and trust me on this..."

"Can't, Gracie." He wished like hell he could, if only because she wanted it so badly. But he had Emma to answer to for one thing, his conscience for another. And he had to, wanted to, look out for her.

"I thought not. Bye, Ben."

He let out a groan. He hadn't wanted it to come to this, but she'd left him with no choice. He reached for the hose behind him. "Grace." He called her back, banking on her good manners to kick in.

They did and she turned to face him. "What?" She raised her hands outward, the action pulling the white jersey taut across her chest. "It's called getting back in the saddle, Ben. Facing your fears. I can't do that with a bodyguard by my side."

She was right. But he still couldn't let her go alone. "You said you used to hand-wash cars with your brother?"

"Is there a point to this other than stalling me?" She

tipped her head to the side and her blond ponytail swiped her shoulders.

He shrugged. "I just wanted to remind you of the fun times in your childhood." With remorse but not regret, he raised the hose and turned it on her.

The cold water hit her chest and Grace let out a shriek. Then she leaped forward and made a grab for the hose, only Ben was faster. He turned out of the way just as she managed to get a hand locked on the green rubber. She yanked hard and caught him off guard. But the force of the water took the hose out of his hands. It hit the ground, moving around like a snake, saturating them both.

Grace knew she ought to be furious, but she was too busy laughing instead. For those few minutes, she felt young and free, as she had only when she'd hung out with Logan—away from the judge and her mother, their control and social mores.

She yanked her shirt free of the knot she'd made earlier and wrung out the hem while Ben got the hose under control. "Don't think I don't know that was deliberate."

He turned back toward her, his eyes gleaming with amusement and mischief. "You left me no choice." He met her stare briefly before his gaze darted lower.

She followed his lead and looked down, only to find her pure lace bra was completely visible through the wet T-shirt. A fact Ben hadn't missed, if the darkening of his irises was any indication. A breeze blew through the air, chilling her wet skin. Her darkened nipples pulled into tight peaks before her eyes—and Ben's steely gaze. That control was shot to hell, if she had to take a guess.

And Grace couldn't say she'd miss it. Obviously she'd captured his attention and no matter how awkward she felt, darned if she was going to fold her arms over her chest and ruin the moment. A bad girl wouldn't miss this opportunity.

"We all have choices, Ben." They both knew she spoke more of the electricity between them and what he chose to do—or not do—about it.

He folded his arms across his broad chest. "And I'm choosing to walk away before this gets out of hand." He turned toward the car. Away from her.

But Grace wasn't giving in. Not now. She grabbed for his wrist. "What are you running from?" She'd wondered before. Now she had to know.

A steady stream of people had begun to enter and exit the building. "Can we take this somewhere private?" he asked, deliberately staring at her chest. A reminder that if he could see what was so clearly visible, so could anyone else who chose to take a peek.

She refused to let him accomplish his goal—to make *her* uncomfortable enough to do the backing off for him. "Sure thing." She grabbed for the handle of the car and opened the door. She'd left the driver's seat pushed forward and she slid into the back. And waited.

He stared at her in disbelief.

"Are you going to join me? Because I look pretty silly sitting in here by myself."

His glare told her he wasn't amused by her antics. She grinned. "No problem. You can go inside and dry off and I can head downtown as planned."

He narrowed his gaze. "Not dressed like that you're not."

She treated him to her sweetest smile. "Want to test me?" Grace had no intention of going anywhere in her drenched state, except her apartment, and only if Ben went with her. But unless he gave in and crawled into the car for a more personal, intimate conversation, he might just force her hand. And she might find herself walking down the street, giving New York City's residents a view of more than the skyline.

He let out a growl, then slipped into the front seat and turned on the ignition.

"Where are we going?"

He didn't answer. Instead he put the car in gear and drove around the corner, coming to a stop on a side street behind the building. A secluded, quiet area without a steady flow of pedestrian traffic.

"I get it. Privacy." She grinned. "Maybe I was wrong about you. Maybe you aren't running from me after all."

He shut the engine, opened the door and got out long enough to switch positions and join her in the back seat. "Okay, princess. I played the game your way. You got what you wanted. You got me alone." His darkened eyes met hers. "Now what are you going to do with me?"

5

GRACE RECOGNIZED the challenge in Ben's words. He didn't think she had it in her to make the first move. She wouldn't have thought she had it in her, either. But she knew a showdown when she saw one and if she didn't act now, there wouldn't be a later. Suddenly chilled from sitting in a damp shirt, she shivered.

"Cold?" He may have joined her in the back, but he still sat in the opposite corner of the small car.

She nodded. "Good thing I know just how to keep warm."

She moved quickly, before she lost her nerve and hoping to catch him off guard, she climbed onto his lap. Face-to-face, she placed her knees on either side of his legs and settled herself into the juncture of his thighs.

He exhaled hard and let out a groan that vibrated through her. "Body heat," she explained. But what she felt went beyond heat. More like a burning blaze and unlike anything she'd ever felt before.

She released any leg muscles that would have held her apart from him until the rising bulge in his jeans nestled snug between her thighs. Damp denim against damp denim suddenly didn't matter.

He clenched his jaw, fighting the obvious pleasure brought by their intimate contact. "Do you always get what you want, princess?"

She shook her head. "Good try, but I'm not biting." Grace recognized the ploy to place distance between them. No way would she let him use her weakness to push her away again.

"How so?" He raised an eyebrow and met her gaze, attempting to appear unaffected.

But she knew better. She'd caught the flicker of regret at his words in his dark eyes. "Let's just say I may have been privileged, but I rarely got what I really wanted." Fewer *things* and more caring. "On the other hand, I get the feeling you tend to get what you desire."

"Not while I was growing up. We weren't exactly in your league." His jaw clenched tight.

"Not many families are and, believe me, you ought to consider yourself lucky. Did you have love?" The word hovered between them.

He nodded.

"Then you were much more privileged than I ever was. And Ben, I should warn you—I may not have gotten what I wanted then..."

"But you plan to get it now?"

She nodded. "I most certainly do."

His eyes smoldered with the same flame threatening to consume her, but instead of pulling her into the kiss she desired, he clenched his hands into fists at his sides.

She shook her head and admitted to herself she'd have preferred he took control and kissed her senseless, but by holding back he was teaching her important lessons on experimenting and being bold.

She let out an exaggerated sigh. "I can do this the hard way or the easy way. With your cooperation or without it. Either way I have no doubt I'll eventually get what we both want." She raised her hands and placed them on his bare chest.

That initial move was difficult but now that she'd touched his skin, the rest came a bit easier. She shut her eyes for only a moment, savoring the feel of his heated flesh beneath her palms. Then, taking advantage, she grazed his nipples with her thumbs, until they'd distended into hard peaks.

His hips jerked upward and she sucked in a breath at the same time an unexpected rising swell of desire flooded through her.

New. The sensations he aroused were new and exciting. She moistened her lips with her tongue. "Before I go with the more aggressive approach, you're going to have to tell me why you're holding back."

A smile twitched at his lips. "You're telling me you can actually get *more* aggressive?" His hands came to rest at her hips. "'Cause from where I'm sitting, princess, this is as aggressive as it gets."

She glanced down at their nearly joined bodies.

"Yeah, it is pretty masterful of me, isn't it?" She grinned, pleased with how quickly she was learning.

His hands slid beneath her shirt and inched upward, until his palms settled on the bare skin by her rib cage and his thumbs grazed the lower swell of her breasts. She knew he was attempting to scare her off again. Either that or make her give in to whatever pleasure *he* had in mind. As tempting as that thought was, Grace had her own agenda. By sheer strength of will alone, she kept her eyelids open and refused to give in.

"Masterful women turn me on." His hands moved higher as his fingertips brushed her nipples, a brief, teasing touch that left her wanting more.

"So you like dominant women, do you?" She brushed a fingertip down his cheek and nearly lost herself in his seductive gaze.

"Oh, yeah."

Taking a wild guess at what he'd like, she clamped her thighs together and pushed her hips forward, holding his powerful erection hostage to her whims. He groaned and she discovered what he liked, she enjoyed, too.

"I can play the same game you can," she said on a ragged breath and hoped she wasn't lying. "I can tease and torment as long as you can, probably longer. And I will. Until I know why the push and pull. Why you've been fighting the attraction between us."

"You don't want much, do you?" Just his soul, Ben

thought. Her damp heat surrounded him and she'd begun a steady clenching of her pelvic muscles that had him grinding his teeth and nearly sent him over the edge.

But the rational part of him didn't blame her for her confusion and understood the need to resort to dominant tactics. And she was good at them. So good that in another second, he'd be blurting out all his secrets. Something that wouldn't do either of them any good and would deny them both what they desperately desired: each other.

Warm brown eyes met his. "I want you, Ben." But he saw the insecurity hovering in the darkened depths and respected that, although she played a game, the act and the feelings were obviously new for her, too.

His body shook from the effort of holding back, from the exertion of *not* taking her into his arms and kissing her senseless, then stripping off those wet clothes and burying himself deep inside her.

He forced himself to think about what her statement implied. She wanted him, but she didn't know who he really was. She desired answers to why he held back, yet he couldn't tell her he was maintaining his distance for the sake of his job. And for her grandmother's sake.

So he opted for the safest route. "I don't do commitments."

At least he never had before. No woman had lasted longer than a month, tops. Between work and caring for his ailing mother, he'd never had the time to make the effort it took for a relationship to last. He glanced at Grace. Or maybe no woman had interested him enough, fascinated him enough.

She shrugged. "It's been a while since I've had one of my own. And I don't recall asking you for any commitments." She ran one fingernail down his chest, slowing down at the thin line of hair from his navel into the waistband of his jeans.

The tingling sensation set his already raw nerve endings aflame. He swallowed hard. "You might not be asking, but you're entitled to them."

"I think I know best what I want." She worked at the clasp on his fly. "What I need." She popped open the button of his jeans. "What I *deserve.*"

He grabbed her wrist in his hand. His body was strung tight while his mind wandered in varied directions. He could give in, give them both what they desired and he could walk away in the end. But his conscience kicked in, telling him he couldn't selfishly take, while lying to her at the same time.

If he wanted to deceive himself, he could say giving in had professional benefits. A temporary relationship with Grace enabled him to protect her when she was on the streets, in the park. She'd fight him accompanying her under any circumstances but, as a couple, he'd have a chance to remain by her side during the time he was in Emma's employ. A chance to discover who was out to get her, and why.

But why lie? He *wanted* to protect her, apart from

doing his job. When he left in a few short weeks, he wanted to leave her safe. And giving in to her now would help him in his cause, help him be close to her in the time they had left. "You deserve the best."

She arched her back and leaned closer. The effect was more intimate body contact—if such a thing were possible. Her feminine mound nestled against his straining erection.

She glanced down at their intertwined hands. "Then you need to let go of me." Her voice came out a breathless whisper.

He released his grip, wondering just how far she would go. But he had to touch her. He needed the contact too badly. Reaching out, he grabbed for her ponytail, freeing the delicate strands from confinement. Blond hair sifted over her shoulders and grazed her face.

"I'm all yours, princess." He leaned his head back against the seat, wanting to get a better look at her. Her cheeks were flushed and her brown eyes were alive with delight...and determination.

She wiggled backward, each not-so-subtle movement putting a strain on his erection. She hesitated and he felt her indecision. He waited, knowing it was her choice.

And then she made it, pulling down on his zipper with an excruciatingly slow motion, making sure her hand cupped and molded his arousal with each incremental move downward.

Ben thought he knew all about foreplay. He

thought he knew how to control himself, but her dainty yet deliberate maneuvers were bringing him closer to the edge than ever before in his life and the anticipation of what she planned next was killing him.

"You'd better be sure you know what you're doing," he said through tightly clenched teeth.

She flipped her mane of hair over her shoulder and glanced up. "Are you questioning my prowess?" Her lips lifted into a provocative grin, but her eyes held questions.

"I'd be a fool to deny the obvious."

As if his words had given her permission, she then edged the zipper down completely. With one hand, she reached inside his open jeans and with a little dexterity, she freed his erection.

He let out a slow groan. "I just want to make sure you know what you're getting yourself into."

"Like you said, it'd be ridiculous to deny the obvious." She ran her palm up and down his rigid shaft in a move more experimental than sure. "And besides, you drove us into a secluded alley behind the building. No one's going to see us."

He let out a groan. She obviously meant what she said. She wanted to play with fire. And since he'd already made his decision not to back off, the control he'd held on to snapped.

Between them, they made fast work of her jeans. Despite the cramped quarters, somehow they got them unsnapped and down over her hips until they went flying to the other side of the car.

Clad only in a wet T-shirt and a mere scrap of silk, Grace sat on her knees beside him. He took in her pale skin and the rounded curves beneath the wet material and let out an approving whistle.

Her cheeks burned with embarrassment. Fire. "I take it you like what you see?" she asked, her eyes hopeful.

The question was more telling than the spurts of bravado she'd been exhibiting. She might know what she wanted but she wasn't certain of his approval. She wasn't certain of him.

Ben might not be able to give her the whole honest truth, but he could give her this. He crooked a finger her way. "Come here, Grace."

"Not princess?" she asked lightly. Too lightly.

He hadn't realized just how important the distinction was to her. He met her gaze. "I want." Without glancing down, he added, "I think you know how much. And I also know *who* I want and it's *Grace*. Not someone I imagine you to be, but you. My gorgeous, sexy neighbor." He crooked his finger once more. "So how long are you going to make me wait?"

Her eyes gleamed with approval before she crawled back into his lap, only this time, just a thin barrier of silk separated their wanting flesh. And he felt her. Every hot inch of his erection was enveloped by moist warmth, dewy wetness. "Sweet heaven, you feel good."

"You're not so bad yourself." She squeezed her legs together and succeeded in enhancing the powerful sensations building within him.

He grabbed the back of her neck in his hand. "Just this once I hope you don't mind if I take charge." Without waiting for an answer, he pulled her close and sealed her lips with his.

Before they went further, he'd wanted to taste the sweetness of her mouth, and the promise of more to come. He'd needed the intimacy of this kiss.

A loud rapping on the window startled them and she jumped, nearly dislodging herself from his lap. He grabbed her hips to keep her on top of him. Although whoever was out there couldn't possibly see Grace thanks to the combination of steamed up windows and the angle in which he'd pulled the car, he still didn't want to expose any more of them than necessary.

"Take it inside." Ben recognized their landlord's voice and raucous laugh. No doubt Grace did as well.

With an embarrassed groan, she reached for her pants. Ben muttered a curse and leaned his head back against the seat. No matter how much he'd enjoyed, he couldn't deny a part of him welcomed the interruption.

Because when the alarm bells had gone off in his head, he had been too far gone to listen.

GRACE TURNED ON THE SHOWER. She glanced at the faucet and debated—hot water to stop the chill on her damp skin or cold water to douse the fire raging inside her? After five minutes of both, she realized neither would help. Cold water pelted her sensitized skin, and chafed her still-puckered nipples until they ached for Ben's soothing touch. Hot water let steam invade the room, reminding her of the damp moisture they'd created together inside Ben's hot and steamy car.

Her body was alive with sensation and there was nothing that could change it—except Ben. And he'd disappeared into his own apartment with the lame excuse that he had to take a shower. She wished they could have taken one together—it would have been a first for her. One she'd have liked to experience with Ben.

She stepped out and wrapped a towel around her, knowing she wasn't ready for that kind of step. For as much as she'd gone looking for sexual awareness, she'd found so much more...too much more. Beyond discovering her capability to be brazen and wanton around a man, she'd learned much about Ben, and herself.

She craved caring and he knew how to provide it. But, Grace reminded herself, her time with Ben was limited. One month in duration, and by her own agreement, they were involved in nothing more than a casual, no-strings affair. It was too bad because Logan and Catherine would love his down-to-earth charm.

Whoa. She paused in wiping down her legs with the

fluffy towel. She was getting way ahead of herself here. Ben had no intention of sticking around or being a part of her life and, besides, what made her think she would even want him to? She shouldn't even be thinking about what-ifs.

The jarring ring of the telephone saved her from any more analysis. She grabbed for the portable phone she'd left on the counter by the sink. "Hello?"

"Finally. Do you have any idea what it's like getting through to you?"

Grace smiled. "Hi, Gran. I'm sorry I haven't gotten back to you. I've been..." Preoccupied seducing a man. Her smile turned to a full-fledged grin. "Busy."

"Too busy to call your grandmother and let her know you're okay?"

"You're right and I'm sorry."

Emma let out a loud exhale. "Well, that took the wind out of my sails."

Grace chuckled. "I really miss you, Gran."

"Then come visit."

"I...will. Just give me some time to work out my schedule." Like a couple of weeks, once Ben walked out of her life. Grace had a hunch she'd be needing her grandmother's TLC more than ever then.

"That's wonderful. You haven't so much as been willing to consider it since Logan's wedding and that was over a year ago."

She sat down on the edge of the closed toilet seat and sighed. "My life is changing. I can't explain it to you now, but I'm feeling better about things. About me."

"No reason why you shouldn't. You're the best. Now tell me, why the change. New job?"

"That's part of it." Grace hadn't filled Emma in on all the details in her posttrust fund life because she wanted to have things settled. Wanted to know she *could* get by on her own before coming home or sharing her new experiences.

"New guy?"

"Maybe."

Her grandmother let out a long-suffering sigh. "Well, fine. Keep up the silent routine. Just make sure he treats you right on your birthday. And before you get all huffy on me, I'm not talking about expensive gifts. There're plenty of things you can do on a shoestring budget. Why, I hear those sex shops in the city are quite reasonable."

"*Gran!*" Despite all she'd done today with Ben, a heated flush crept up her cheeks at her grandmother's risqué comment.

Emma sniffed into the phone. "When did you and your brother turn into such prudes? I take it you haven't used the bath soaps and candles I sent you for your birthday?"

Grace laughed, refusing to answer. Both she and Logan had grown used to their grandmother's outrageousness years ago. It was Grace's father, the judge, who never understood his mother and constantly threatened to put her in a home. But since neither Logan nor Grace would allow such a thing, he blustered but backed off. As long as Emma didn't publicly create a scandal, Judge Montgomery was satisfied.

"So how are Logan and Cat and the little princess?" Grace asked.

"Perfect, of course. And since you won't come see them, they're talking about coming to visit you. But now that you say you're coming home..."

"Let's take it one step at a time, Gran, okay? I've got to go now. I love you."

"I love you, too. And whoever this guy is, don't act all prim and proper around him. It isn't a turn-on. Bye, dear."

Grace rolled her eyes and hit the Power button on the phone. She thought of herself earlier today in the back seat of Ben's Mustang. Pants beside her on the back seat, knees spread across Ben's lap, his erection nudging at her feminine dampness, and the look of pure ecstasy on his face. A tremor of awareness traveled through her, settling in the empty place between her thighs, the place that longed to be filled—by Ben.

She hadn't been prim and proper this afternoon. Not at all. She'd been downright bad. And she wanted to be naughty again. Amazing that an eighty-something-year-old was giving Grace advice on her sex life.

And it was advice she was already following. If Grace didn't know better, she'd think her grandmother knew Ben.

GRACE WAS TROUBLE, Ben thought. But not more trouble than she was worth, and that was the problem. He'd no sooner jumped out of the cold shower than the daytime doorman had called to inform him Grace was on her way down to the lobby. He hated having to resort to surveillance tactics, but she'd left him no choice.

So he'd waited until she'd gotten into the elevator and then hightailed it down the stairs.

"She went that way." The doorman pointed left, a huge grin on his face.

"Glad you find this amusing," Ben muttered. He followed her out of the building, unable to tear his gaze from the sassy sway of her behind in tight, white denim. He waited around the corner while she went into Starbucks, and watched as she disappeared into the subway entrance, coffee in hand, before he grabbed a cab and headed to the park.

He didn't relish a confrontation and planned to stay out of sight. That way he figured he could keep an eye on her and anyone else doing the same. His sole consolation lay in the fact that she hadn't brought her camera and was a less conspicuous target. But as she rounded the corner by the basketball courts, her blond hair gleamed in the sunshine and her regal form made her stand out in a crowd. Grace was a walking target just by virtue of who she was.

She entered the playground where a group of women sat on a park bench while their children played on the swings and with each other. There wasn't a free seat, but Grace didn't hesitate. She joined them on the ground beside a dark-haired woman, without a thought or care to the white jeans she wore.

Ben didn't know why he was surprised. Grace was as down-to-earth as they came. Too much so for a woman raised in the Montgomery mansion he'd visited a few weeks earlier. But the woman he'd come to know was more at home sitting in the dirt than she was tiptoeing on freshly waxed floors. And she didn't seem to put off the women who'd accepted her into their circle.

Certain her back was to him, he made his way over to the fence and rested his hands on top until the cold bite of metal dug into his skin. She'd kicked her feet out in front of her and leaned back on her elbows, every inch of her relaxed and unwound.

In contrast, his body was still strung tight. He hadn't been kidding when he'd told her masterful women turned him on. What he'd omitted was that it was *her* mastery that did it to him. He'd never encountered such an erotic combination of innocence and seduction in one delectable package. Never had that kind of wide-eyed determination focused solely on him.

A child's shriek rent the air and snapped Ben out of his reverie. He jerked his gaze toward the swings and a set of monkey bars behind. A young kid hung upside down from his legs on one of the bars that were meant to be swung across. A young mother rose, but Grace jumped up and placed a hand on her arm. The woman nodded and Grace ran over in her place, rescuing the upside-down child from all sorts of possible disasters. She set the kid down on his feet, but instead of running off to play, he jumped up and grabbed Grace around the neck, hugging her hard. Apparently they weren't strangers and she lifted him so his legs wrapped around her waist. She paused to ruffle his hair before bringing him back to his waiting mother.

An unexpected lump formed in Ben's throat. He fought it, he tried to swallow it, but the damn thing remained. He recalled similar incidents in his childhood—usually on Sundays, his mother's only day off. No matter how exhausted, she'd take him to a neighborhood park, pack a picnic lunch and set him loose to play. She'd laugh, she'd watch, she'd mend his scrapes and wipe the tears a macho boy didn't want to show.

Just as Grace was doing now. And he knew for certain she had motherly instincts, even if she hadn't once mentioned the desire for family. Hell, she was running so hard from her own family he'd bet she was burying this desire, too. But he'd also bet it existed. Just, he now realized, as it existed for him.

So much of Ben's job was based on sight, perception and instinct. And right now, his were screaming about the danger this woman posed. To his life, his sanity...his heart.

He'd seen many sides of her: the disheveled woman with bags of groceries, the partner who'd helped him wash his car without complaint and the princess in the marble-and-crystal palace. But the Grace Montgomery with a child hanging around her neck was more of a threat to Ben than the seductive siren who'd sat nearly naked on his lap.

Feeling like an intruder in her life as well as his own, he turned away. But not before Grace looked toward him and her gaze seemed to zero in. He couldn't be certain she'd seen him.

But if she had, he'd know soon enough.

GRACE REREAD THE NOTE in her hand. *Play it smart. Don't come back. Or else.* With shaking hands, she dumped the paper into the trash by her bed. Whoever was harassing her had stooped low enough to use a child to deliver his threats. Grace recalled the moment Kurt had given her the innocent-looking note— about the same time she'd caught sight of Ben.

And it was Ben she focused on now. The threats wouldn't go away any more than her need to take pictures and she'd have to deal with both. Later.

Grace exited the building. She knew she wasn't

playing fair. But then again, had Ben played fair when he'd followed her earlier? He thought she hadn't noticed when he'd exited the side entrance to the building, but she had.

She wasn't as angry as she ought to be considering he hadn't trusted her enough to go out on her own. He'd followed her because he was concerned, yet he'd given her the freedom to do as she pleased, with the security of knowing he was a shout away should trouble find her.

But when the note had been delivered, Grace hadn't yelled for Ben. She'd kept it from him because he'd overreact. He'd fight her need to return to the place she loved best, the place that helped her to find her place in the world.

She wasn't angry that Ben felt the need to follow her and she understood his reasons—but she did plan on teaching him a lesson. One he wouldn't soon forget.

After her fright at the park, she'd thrown her energies into preparing Ben's surprise for the evening. She cleaned up and took yet another shower, making certain to use the bath soaps and lotions Emma had sent her as part of her birthday present—the ones her grandmother claimed had so-called aphrodisiac powers, though how Emma knew about such things was something Grace had no desire to question further.

She put the finishing touches on her apartment,

slipped into an outfit designed to send Ben over the edge and headed out the door.

NOT AGAIN. BEN HADN'T recovered from Grace's last jaunt outdoors when he got the call from the doorman downstairs she was off again. He'd be grateful for Monday when she returned to work and a regimented schedule. In the meantime, if she was out of here, so was he.

Varying his routine, he waited till she got on the elevator, and then took the next one down himself. The doorman had promised to watch out for her, and when Ben got downstairs, he pointed in the direction she'd taken—downtown as he'd feared.

Ben exited the double doors and glanced in the direction the doorman had gestured. Why the hell did she have to hit that part of town in the evening? When she was more likely to find trouble…definitely, dressed like that.

He recognized her even from behind. Especially from behind. The blond hair pulled up with strands brushing her shoulders, the pale skin on her back, the long shapely legs and lithe body—all visible thanks to the slender tank-type two-piece top and short skirt she wore.

He sucked in an audible breath. He had no idea where she was headed, but she wasn't going alone. And she damn sure better not be meeting someone male.

He followed her into the subway, unable to stop

staring. Unable to stop fantasizing about those long legs and how they'd feel wrapped around him again, only this time there'd be no barriers between them. No scrap of silk acting as a shield between her damp heat and the arousal she inspired. Dressed the way she was, he couldn't imagine her ultimate destination, other than a date. Ben cursed and swore to himself. Date or not, no other man would come between them.

He broke into a heated sweat that had nothing to do with the hot and humid subway car they entered. He watched from behind a crowd as Grace twirled a blond strand around one finger, wishing she'd tangle those hands in his hair. He grew impossibly hotter as he mentally removed himself from the subway and placed himself back into the Mustang. His breathing became shallow as he remembered their mingled breaths steaming up the windows and heating the re-cycled air in the back of the car.

The squeal of the brakes as they came to a halt jolted Ben back into reality in time for him to rise and follow Grace's exit from the subway car. She walked up the stairs and into the street, but to his surprise, in-stead of turning toward the park, she rounded the corner and headed back into the subway station that would return her to the Murray Hill neighborhood where she lived.

And in the instant she settled herself into a seat and turned back to wave at him in between the crowds of people, Ben knew. He'd been had.

He waved back. What else could he do?

She smiled, her glossy red lips turned upward in an amused grin. He wanted to kiss those lips and taste the sweet recesses of her mouth, but since she was toying with him, he doubted he'd be doing any of those things any time soon. And though he should be grateful, he'd already accepted an intimate relationship between them was inevitable. It was his guilt and inner torment he hadn't come to terms with.

But when she sidled up to him, so close he could inhale her fragrant scent over the other less appealing smells in the musty car, he couldn't focus on anything but Grace.

Like any other passenger, she grabbed the hanging strap next to his. But she wasn't any other woman. She was the one who had him tied in knots. The one who had lured him into her trap and enticed him to succumb to wiles he'd guess she was just discovering she possessed.

"I take it you aren't going anywhere special?" he asked.

"Nope."

"Just taking a ride for the hell of it then?"

When she remained silent, he glanced down, then up again, from her high heels and long legs, to the short hem on her enticing nude-colored outfit. His hands itched to lift the bottom a notch and see if her undergarments looked as sultry and sexy as the lady herself. "No hot date?"

"Now that depends." She twirled a stray tendril

around her finger. He'd bet the gesture was a deliberate attempt to be provocative.

It worked. Grace was doing a damn good job of working him up and keeping him captivated. No doubt about it, everything about her turned him on. "Depends on what?"

"You're pretty hot when you're not following me around like I'm a kid who can't be trusted to go out on my own."

He knew better than to get into the debate about why he'd tailed her. Instead he addressed the more important issue at hand. "So you think I'm hot?"

She tipped her head to the side. "I'm not sure I like that cocky smile."

"Oh, I think you do."

Her arousing laugh echoed inside the crowded car. "You're all male, I'll give you that."

The subway jarred to a halt and a majority of the passengers disembarked at the stop, leaving them alone in the nearly empty car. "Want to sit?"

She shook her head. "No, thank you. I'd rather stay here. This close to you." Her hip brushed against him as the subway jerked forward once more.

His palms grew damp, making it difficult to hang on to the strap.

"Now where were we?" She pursed those red lips in thought. "Oh, yes. You. Being all male." The pucker turned into a grin. "From these strong eyebrows to those pouty lips, you're one extremely *sexy* man." She drew a line down the side of his face, then traced his lips with a newly polished red fingernail. Her finger lingered on his mouth for another few seconds before she rested her hand against her hip. Just looking at how the red on her nails matched the red on her lips caused a quickening in his gut.

He knew he'd have noticed if she'd worn that flaming red shade before. The color was sexy enough to bring a man to his knees. The notion made him nervous as hell and he glanced up, but he couldn't tear his gaze from her smoky one.

Nor could he stop the pull running from his tingling lips to his hard arousal. "This is payback for following you, isn't it?" His voice was rough with wanting.

"Now that would be petty."

An evasive answer at best, he thought. And since the trip was obviously planned, he couldn't help but wonder what else she had in store. Add to that she still hadn't answered his question. "Are you hinting that *I* might be your date?"

A smoldering heat darkened her gaze as she leaned closer. "It's a possibility—if you'll agree not to treat me like a child."

His gaze slipped downward to her cleavage, visible from his slightly taller vantage point. Her rounded flesh swelled over cream-colored lace, making him drool. "You're anything but a child, Gracie."

"Nice of you to notice."

"You know I had no choice but to provide backup for you, just in case."

She averted her gaze for an instant before touching his cheek with her hand. "Yes, I know. You're a good man, Ben. You're concerned about me and I appreciate that. But I want you to treat me like a woman. And that means I just might have to remind you how much of a woman I can be."

He glanced around. The only few passengers left were seated, involved in conversation or reading the paper. He and Grace might as well have been alone.

"Trust me, Grace, I have no doubt just how much woman you are." Adrenaline rushed through him and his heart beat too fast in his chest.

"The question is, can you handle me?"

"Oh, I think I'm up to the challenge." Since she was taking full advantage, how could he not do the same? "Feel what you do to me." He brushed up against her, making sure the rigidity of his arousal pressed hard and insistent against her leg.

She sucked in a startled breath.

Turning the tables on her felt too good. He was enjoying this too much. But at the moment, he didn't give a damn. And, he reminded himself without listing the reasons again, he'd already made up his mind to go with her lead—and his desire.

He knew all too well where they were headed. And so did she, unless her shocked silence indicated she'd changed her mind.

Grace swallowed hard. Heat seared her thigh where his erection thrust against her leg, reminding her of exactly what she'd put into motion. The ultimate seduction, she thought.

"It's not too late to change your mind." His husky voice reverberated in her ear. "'Course I'll be disappointed, but I'd understand. My mother raised a gentleman."

"She did, huh?"

"Not that you'd know it by looking at me, but yes, she did."

She tilted her head. "Well, tell her she did a fine job."

"I will. She'll appreciate it, too. She doesn't get much outside information anymore."

Honest information willingly given for the first time. Grace was grateful. "You make it sound like she lives in prison."

"They call it an independent living facility but her eyesight's going, so the independent part no longer fits. She doesn't get out much anymore."

Grace heard the love and affection in his tone for the woman who'd raised him. Yet another thing to like and admire about this man. "But I'll bet she's got you."

"Every Sunday afternoon and whenever else I can drop by."

Her heart opened toward him even more. First the kids downtown and now his mother. "You're special," she murmured.

It touched her deeply to know he had yet another soft spot. This man, the one she'd picked to help discover and release her inner self, was so much more than just a sexy neighbor.

"You're pretty special yourself."

"What makes you say that?"

"For one thing, you've polished your investigating skills in a short time."

She laughed, knowing she'd been caught prying into his life and not caring a bit. "What else?" She'd already decided she was shameless when it came to Ben. Why not push for more compliments? She could use them to bolster her courage.

"You're an incredible woman." He squeezed her hand tight in his.

That simple gesture, along with his support, admiration and respect, solidified her feelings for him. Ben was exactly what she saw, no more, no less. But most importantly, and the one thing that made him the perfect man at this point in her life, was that he respected Grace Montgomery, apart from her family money or family name. Ben Callahan was an honest man, one worlds apart from the Montgomery influence.

Without warning, the subway came to a jarring halt. She lost her balance and fell against his hard male body. His arms grabbed her around the waist. Enveloped in his warmth, surrounded by his scent, Grace wondered who was the seducer and who was the one being seduced.

"I think that's our cue."

She straightened and smoothed her outfit at the

waist. "I think you're right." The doors opened and she preceded him out of the subway. Hands shaking, heart hammering, she waited for him to meet her on the platform.

With his razor stubble, his worn jeans and ripped sweatshirt, he was her rebel. The antithesis of everyone and everything she'd turned her back on, Ben epitomized all she'd wanted to be and never had the courage to reach out for—until now.

She licked her lips, tasting gloss and wishing she tasted him. She looked into his eyes, seeing a man she desired and a man she respected. Despite her promise of no strings, she wasn't a casual sex type of person and she wouldn't have chosen Ben if all he could give was a glimpse into her passionate side. He had depth and offered her so much more.

"Ready when you are," she said.

"You already welcomed me to the building." He reached out and touched her cheek. "Anything else is icing on the cake."

She inhaled an unsteady breath. "So I guess the question is, are you ready to welcome me to your bed?" Who was this shameless woman who had brazenly propositioned Ben Callahan? Grace didn't recognize her.

But she liked her—a lot.

And she had Ben to thank for bringing out this wanton side of her. For introducing her to Grace Montgomery, the woman. And she knew exactly how to repay him.

7

THE TRAIN PULLED OUT behind them. Standing on the platform, Ben took her hand. Her palms were damp, one of the few signs she was nervous about this seduction. The desire between them was mutual but he could tell by her question she wasn't as secure as she'd have him believe.

The only way to convince her was to show her. Without hesitation, he swept her into his arms and off her feet.

"What do you think you're doing?" The note of outrage in her voice was rendered ineffective by the upturned corners of her mouth.

He couldn't draw his gaze from those moist, wet lips. "I'm answering your question. Hell, yes, I want you in my bed," he said, and lowered his lips to hers.

Her touch was warm and welcoming at first and immediately turned hot and devouring. The moist gloss let her coated lips slide over his in an erotic caress the likes of which he'd never felt before. As he stroked the heated recesses of her mouth with his tongue, she massaged his lips with hers. Every moist stroke sent blazing darts of fire to his groin.

He'd wanted to taste that mouth. Now that he had,

he couldn't get enough. But they were in a public place where he was sure they were creating a free show. With an agonized groan, one echoed silently by each part of his body, he somehow managed to lift his head and rest his forehead against hers.

"Not bad." She sounded out of breath and extremely pleased.

"Yeah, well, I did my best."

Her eyes met his and those moist lips turned upward into a grin. "I'll be damned. It works." She traced his mouth with her fingertip sending his already overheated body into a frenzy of need.

"What's that?"

"I bought this lipstick just for you. The slogan read, color stays on your lips not his." The pad of her finger lingered on the center of his bottom lip, teasing him with a featherlight touch.

He couldn't resist and grazed her skin with his teeth. He tasted warm salty flesh—tasted Grace—and groaned.

"We've got to get out of here," she murmured.

"No kidding." He started for the exit of the subway, ignoring the curious onlookers and the occasional snickers. He knew he'd taken the caveman thing too far, but this woman drove him to utter distraction.

"I can walk."

"I'm sure you can." He continued through the turnstile and up the short flight of stairs.

"But you have no intention of allowing it?"

He answered with a short grunt and kept walking. She'd already proven her mastery at seduction.

Considering that sexy outfit she wore and the stares given her by other men, she should be glad he hadn't banged her over the head and dragged her home by her hair the way his primitive ancestors would have. No doubt, she'd intended to rouse his more savage instincts with this plan and she'd succeeded. Now she could live with the consequences. They were only a short block from the building. The faster he got her home, the better off they'd both be.

She threaded her fingers through his hair. "You know, if you insist on keeping this up, I might as well enjoy it."

He recognized the playful threat in her words. "Go ahead. Your enjoyment is exactly what I have in mind."

She nestled her face between his chin and shoulder. The fragrant scent of her hair assaulted his senses. The soft feel of her skin and her warm breath against his neck gave him a preview of what was to come when he got her alone. Cool sheets, warm bodies, the sensual glide of damp skin—his over hers, hers over his.

He swept her through the open door to the lobby of the building and past the chuckling doorman.

"I'm not sure I'll ever live that down," she said.

He laughed. "And I'm certain it'll do wonders for my reputation."

She shook her head. "You're going to have to pay for that."

"Promises, promises." He hit the button on the elevator. Thankfully it opened without delay. He stepped inside and the doors glided to a close behind them.

No sooner had he pressed the button for their floor than she nuzzled close to his cheek again, only this time, she bit down on his earlobe, sending shock waves through his system. His heart pounded hard in his chest, a fast and furious beat of arousal and anticipation.

By the time they got to the hall outside the apartments, he could barely stand the wait.

"My place work for you?" she asked, her voice as breathless as he felt.

"Since mine's not really mine, yours is fine." He'd much rather be in a place that smelled and felt like Grace than one as unfamiliar as his temporary residence. Besides he didn't need the reminder of his deception marring his time with this special woman.

He put the issue out of his mind. "Keys?" he asked.

She bit down on her lower lip. "It's unlocked."

He opened his mouth to yell but she beat him to it. "Don't go and lecture me, Ben. I had no place to hide keys on me. Besides you've been watching my every move. You've probably even got the security cameras trained on my door."

Another subject he'd avoid. There were too damn

many. "Just don't do it again," he muttered and grabbed for the doorknob.

"Wait."

He met her gaze. Her eyes were opened wide and brimming with an emotion he couldn't name.

"Second thoughts?" Because he'd respect them in an instant, difficult as it would be. In the end, she might be doing herself a favor if she backed out now.

She shook her head. "It's just that I obviously planned this, but it's not an everyday thing for me. And I just wanted to make sure...I mean, I know this is going to sound silly, but...will you respect me in the morning?" Her cheeks flushed a bright shade of pink.

"I'll more than respect you, Gracie." That was his biggest fear—how deeply she drew him in.

He twisted open the doorknob and let them inside, walking into the short entryway with her still in his arms. The flickering candles took Ben by surprise. The small votives had been strategically placed around a room ideal for seduction. A stimulating scent he couldn't name, but one that aroused his senses, surrounded him. He now knew what she meant when she said she'd planned this, and he was touched by the effort and thought she'd put into their first time together.

"Incredible," he whispered in her ear. He lowered her to the floor, letting her body slide against his, letting her feel how much he wanted her.

"Yes, you are."

He chuckled, but his laughter ceased as she molded herself to him. Her legs aligned with his and her feminine mound settled against the rounded bulge in his jeans. With her bracketed in his arms, flush against him, all thoughts fled, replaced by a sizzling heat and a pounding of desire.

"You went to a lot of trouble for us, Gracie." He let his hands sweep into her hair, freeing the strands from confinement and luxuriating in their silken feel.

She smiled. "I'm glad you noticed. I had the doorman come in and light them while we were gone. See why I didn't need keys?"

Grace stepped back and grabbed his hand. Only the knowledge that they wouldn't be apart for long allowed him to separate their bodies, to remove himself from the heated cocoon of desire, long enough to follow her into the atmosphere she'd created.

The glow from the candles created a warmth and intimacy he'd never before experienced. With the pleated shades drawn closed but left open on top, the oncoming of dusk filtered through the window. The dimly lit candles provided the only other light in the room. He inhaled and caught that intoxicating scent again, one he'd never forget.

She walked over to the table where she'd set up an array of sensual treats from which they could choose. With one hand, she swept the expanse of the delight-filled table—a vase of freshly bought roses and a selection of jars, creams and oils.

"Welcome to my simply sensual seduction," she said, and motioned for him to come near.

She'd been seducing him from the moment they met, yet Ben felt as if he'd been awaiting this moment for much longer. A lifetime.

He came up beside her and wasted no time in cradling her cheeks in his hands and stealing a deep, meaningful kiss, one certain to seal their fate for the night ahead. Her mouth was sweet, so warm and welcoming, Ben nearly lost it right then.

He broke the kiss long enough to free the zipper running down the back of her top. He spread the material with his hands and the fabric fell away, sliding down her arms with little effort and pooling on the floor at their feet.

Taking in the view beneath, he drew in a sharp breath. Nude-colored lingerie covered her full breasts, easing them upward so rounded swells of pale skin provided a tantalizing view. And if that sight weren't enough to bring him to his knees, the material was sheer, nearly translucent, with a hint of shimmer to dazzle him in the candlelight. Darkened nipples, visible through the flimsy material, puckered and hardened beneath his hungry gaze. He traced their dusky outline with the pad of one finger, savoring their unique texture against his hand.

He met her gaze, watching as her pupils dilated with each rotation of his hand and every pinch of his fingers on her hardened flesh. He took it slow, holding himself in check, wanting to savor what they shared—not just the physical but the emotional, too. Because the play of expressions on her face—the ecstasy at his touch and the flush of desire—affected him on a level no woman had ever reached before.

He reached out with his hand and pressed it against her soft breast. His fingers curled, wrapping around her and testing her weight and fullness in his hand. "Like that?" he asked.

"Yes." She let out a slow breath coupled with a ragged moan. "And I like this, too." Her hand slid downward, until her palm rested over his erection.

His hips jerked forward seeking more of her firm touch. The sensual array of objects she'd left for them beckoned to him, but no way could he hold out long enough to make use of them. Not the first time. He'd been waiting for her too long as it was.

A wicked grin touched her lips as she pulled his T-shirt out of the waistband of his jeans. He knew how much she was enjoying this control bit, but it was costing him. He'd already broken into a sweat.

Her fingertips grazed his stomach, then his shoulders as she made fast work of removing his shirt and sending it flying across the room. She dipped her head and placed strategic kisses on his chest. Moist kisses with those red lips. Flickering motions of her agile tongue across his hair-roughened skin, across his nipples. The fiery sensation began where she touched, where she licked, where she nipped with her teeth...and traveled a heated path straight to his groin.

He'd had enough of the playful torment. He edged his fingers beneath the straps of her bra, moving his fingers in a slow downward arc, taking the elastic with him until her arms were bracketed by the thin straps. Then he reached for the front clasp and released the hook, freeing her breasts for his view, his touch, his mouth. He bent his head and pulled one of her nipples between his lips, lapping her skin with his tongue, and tugging none too gently with his teeth, until she writhed with the force of her desire.

His body bucked in kind, but he wanted her so primed and ready that when the joining came she'd feel as if they were made to be together. And apparently she enjoyed his ministrations because she grasped his head in her hands, holding him to her breast in a blatant plea for more. He grazed more insistently with the edge of his teeth and her legs buckled beneath her.

"Easy," he murmured, stopping her fall by sweeping her into his arms once more.

"This is becoming a habit of yours." Her eyes were a deep, dark brown, shaded with desire.

"Can't say I mind. Where to?"

She wrapped her hands around his neck and cuddled close. Her bare and sensitive breasts rasped against his naked chest, and the abrading sensation aroused him even more. "Protection's on the table. We could go to the bedroom—if you make it that far. Personally I don't want to wait."

He let out a low growl. "You finally did it, Gracie."

He took her from being cradled in his arms, to lying flat on her back on the carpeted floor in mere seconds. He hovered over her, his arms on either side of her shoulders, his body levered over hers, feeling predatory and more like his caveman ancestors with each passing second. "You snapped that control I've been hanging on to."

She exhaled a sigh of relief and grinned. "Well, it's about time." She reached out and popped the snap on his jeans and began to tug and twist them downward, impatience showing in her jerky motions. With little difficulty, he yanked them over his hips, briefs along with them, and tossed the garments beside her top.

Grace shook with anticipation. She'd felt the pressure of his body against hers before, but always behind a barrier of clothing, or in cramped quarters in the back seat of his car. Never had she seen him fully erect and aroused as he was now. Her heart began a steady pounding, knowing he wanted her as badly and as desperately as she wanted him. And she did. Never before had she felt such elemental lust for a man. *This* man.

He reached for the condoms on the table and left them beside her on the carpet. Then he knelt on the floor. His heady scent filled her nostrils, and when he met her gaze with his steely one, a rush of liquid moisture pooled between her legs. Without breaking eye contact, he grasped her hips and pulled on the skirt, taking the material down to her knees and then lower, until she was able to kick it off with one foot.

Ben glanced down. And Grace held her breath as he took in her nude, sheer, string-bikini panties. His eyes glazed over. "If I'd known about these, you'd never have made it off the subway." He eased one finger between her skin and the barely-there thread of material holding front and back triangles together, while his other hand covered her feminine mound.

Hot and heavy, his palm eased up then down, gently at first, until the cresting wave hit her without warning and his touch became a harder more insistent branding of his flesh against hers. Her hips rode upward, searching for more of the exquisite pressure, and she let out a shuddering moan of frustration and need.

Ben caught on quick, bearing down with his hand. The rippling of contractions started at the pressure point and circled outward, encompassing her entire body in white-hot spiraling heat. She thrust upward, gyrating against his giving hand. She heard the whimpers, knew they were coming from her throat, and didn't care. Not so long as the amazing waves continued.

Just as the crest began to ease off, just as a hint of awareness began to return, he picked up a circling motion with his palm, a demanding rotation that started the surge of ecstasy all over again.

She didn't think she could take it, not again, not alone, coming alive beneath his touch, but without him deep inside her body. He didn't give her a choice, just continued to take her on a ride she'd never experienced before. His hand worked magic while his fingers cupped her more intimately pushing against the silken, wet barrier of the bikinis she wore. Her climax was just as hard, just as fast, just as long the second time, the sheer force and passion involved taking her by surprise.

Her mind slowly began to clear. His gaze remained steady on hers. A taut but pleased expression settled on his face while his hand remained between her thighs.

"You're so wet, so responsive." His hoarse voice registered in her still sensually fogged brain.

"All for you," she murmured, barely able to speak. But she was finally able to think, and she focused on this man who had given her such intense, singular pleasure. A lump rose in her throat along with an emotion she refused to dissect or name.

His fingers curled deeper, pressed harder against her panties. Pleasure, more sensitized this time, rose fast. *"Again?"* Grace hadn't known it was possible.

"Together this time." She hardly recognized his raspy, desire-laden voice and a ripple of anticipation traveled through her.

He slid out of her reach and straddled her thighs, leaning forward to press a kiss against the triangle of material still covering her.

His breath was warm, his lips hot, and fire licked at her once more. "Ben." His name burst from her lips, an expression of her desire for them to make love.

He understood that she wanted to be filled by him

because he yanked on the thin strap of material, freeing her feminine secrets for him to see. She was hot and she was damp. The cooler air in the apartment touched her already swollen, needy skin and she trembled.

Grasping her thighs in his hands, he exhaled hard, his breathing coming in shallow gasps. "Do you have any idea what you do to me?"

"Show me."

He reached for the condom, tearing at the foil with his teeth and making fast work of protecting them both. A shudder consumed her at the sight, and seconds later his hands were back on her thighs, inching higher. With exact precision, his thumbs moved upward, gliding over her slick folds. And then he nudged his erection inside, solid and strong as he came into her with a single, powerful thrust.

As he filled her body, Grace felt every hot inch, each rigid upward motion. And as he leaned down for a warm, tender kiss, one filled with the mixture of his unique taste and her feminine scent, an unexpected emotion swamped her.

She realized...he had also filled her heart.

A powerful wave of desire rushed through Ben's veins. He closed her hands inside his and raised her arms above her head. The action brought their bodies into more intimate contact, sealing their damp skin together, forcing him deeper inside her. Cocooned in her warmth, cradled in the moist dampness of her passion, Ben wasn't certain where he left off and she began.

He grit his teeth, knowing he was mere seconds away from release. She trembled beneath him, her entire body in a slickened, fevered state identical to his own. Needing the leverage, he released her hands but before he could move, she reached for his shoulders and pushed against him.

"Sit," she whispered, her breath hot against his ear.

Curious, he met her gaze.

"Trust me."

Somehow he stayed inside her as they juggled into the position she'd commanded. Her legs straddled his waist while he sat with her on his lap. Their bodies meshed intimately, his penetration deep, their top halves aligned. Her lush breasts crushed against his chest and her nipples pressed into his skin. The result was the most consuming intimacy he'd ever experienced with a woman, one he'd never forget.

Her wide-eyed gaze met his, telling him she, too, felt the awe-inspiring sense of completeness. "I guess those articles don't lie."

"You're bad, Gracie." He brushed her long strands of hair off her face. A flush of desire along with embarrassment stained her cheeks. He gazed directly into her eyes. Another unique result of their position was the ability to wholly focus on her delicate features. "Have you been reading up on this?"

"Would you believe I discovered the article by accident?'' She moistened her lips with her tongue, a sweeping movement across her full bottom lip.

"Not a chance, sweetheart." He leaned forward for a taste of the dampness she'd created, drawing her lower lip between his teeth and nibbling before letting go. "I'd rather believe you were getting ready for me."

She wrapped his arms around her waist and that threatening wave crested once more. His body shook with the effort of restraint, but he didn't miss the dilation of her pupils or the tremors beginning to engulf her body. She was beyond ready and so was he.

He enclosed his legs around her bottom, pressing his hips against hers. Arching her back, she met his movements, as they began a pulsing, grinding reach for completion. He reached out and cupped her breasts, flattening her nipples against his palms and squeezing her plump flesh with his hands. Without warning, she threw her head back and moaned, bucking her lower body against his. His straining erection slid out a fraction, then back in, deeper, harder than before. Her undulating, frenzied motions drove him mad and he lost control, ceded command of their lovemaking to the wild bucking of her hips and the grinding of her slick body against his own.

He wanted to watch her when she came, wanted to see her face as he exploded inside her, but she caught him off guard. Her climax hit without warning, engulfing her entire body in a quaking release that started inside her, but traveled to him until he was absorbed by the power of his orgasm and consumed by the shuddering vibrations racking her body.

When it was over, he found himself staring into her brown eyes, darkened by need and rounded by wonder. "That was...unbelievable," she said.

And a hell of a lot more, Ben thought. He ought to know. She'd picked the position and it had been incredible, but it didn't allow for retreat. He hadn't counted on the tenderness he'd feel afterward, and now, still enclosed in her moistness, her face mere inches away, he was experiencing a whole host of emotions he was afraid to look at too deeply, afraid of identifying.

"Glad you enjoyed it." He forced a lightness to his voice he didn't feel, but even he heard the strain.

Time to go. He started to push himself backward, but her legs tightened around his waist and the squeezing sensation sent tremors of awareness shooting to his groin, starting the pangs of arousal all over again.

"You don't have to run anywhere. Physically or emotionally, you don't need to withdraw from me." Understanding softened her features and she cradled his face between her palms. "I'm not going to ask or force you into anything other than what we have here. Now. And if I do say so myself, it was pretty darn good." She wiggled her hips provocatively against his.

He let out a groan. "It was great." They were great.

And though he ought to be relieved at her cavalier

acceptance of how little he wanted from her, how little he was willing to offer her, he wasn't—not by a long shot. And a ridiculous pang of regret twisted at his gut.

"Yes, it was great." She leaned closer and her breasts brushed his chest. "And you have nothing to worry about. Frankly I can't see my daddy running after you with a shotgun, so can't you just relax and enjoy the rest of the night?"

He laughed. A brittle laugh because her words cemented what he'd always known. He wasn't worthy of Grace Montgomery and her privileged, elitist background. No father of hers would chase after him, demanding he marry his daughter.

They were different people from divergent, clashing backgrounds—not to mention that he'd entered her life under false pretenses. He couldn't undo his lies any more than she'd forgive him if she knew.

He shook his head. All this damn thinking wasn't like him. And it had to stop. He'd take what he could in the short time they had and walk away. No more analyzing, no more regret.

"Ben?"

He grasped her around the waist, holding her slender hips in his hands and sliding his palms around to her flat belly. She sighed and his fingers dipped lower, until they rested atop the coarser hair and secrets lying beneath. "Enjoying now sounds good to me, Gracie."

"I knew you could be persuaded." She brushed her mouth over his cheek.

He tilted his head toward her table of jars and bath gels. "How about a shower and some more fun?"

"Sounds good. Wickedly good." Her lips lifted upward.

If the smile didn't quite reach her eyes, he refused to acknowledge it. If there were shadows in the brown depths, he refused to look deeper or ask why.

Now, he reminded himself. It was all they had.

8

STEAM, MIXED WITH the arousing scent of jasmine, filled the enclosed space in the bathroom. Grace didn't need any additional aphrodisiac other than Ben to turn her on, but the seductive aroma and the liquid bath gel would heighten what had already been an extraordinary experience.

She wished it didn't have to end. But when the earth-shattering climax had subsided, she'd opened her eyes, taken one look at the panic in Ben's face and known there was no future. Not for them. And though she didn't know exactly why he feared intimacy and commitment, she was perceptive enough to take note of his anxiety and realize if she didn't reassure him and accept *now*, she'd lose whatever time he was still willing to share.

Her lighthearted rhetoric letting him off the hook had been the most difficult words of her life. But they'd accomplished her goal; Ben was still by her side.

She planned on using her pathetic detective skills to uncover the source of his commitment phobia, but not quite yet. She had other treats in store first.

"All ready." She walked to the partially open door

and called out. Ben had offered to blow out the candles to prevent a fire hazard. Suspecting he needed a moment to regroup, she'd agreed.

By the time he joined her in the bathroom, she was standing beneath the pulsating spray, welcoming the hot water sluicing over her sensitized skin. Her shower curtain was see-through with silver stars but they didn't obscure her vision. He entered looking more relaxed than he had minutes earlier. Of course, she planned to allay his concerns and soothe his tension even more.

His body was incredible to gaze upon but she wanted to do much more than look. The play of muscle as he moved and the sexy air that was so much a part of him beckoned to her. And her fingers itched to work themselves up his hard calves, the muscular thighs and bury themselves in the tangle of hair surrounding his erection, which seemed to grow on command beneath her heated stare. She would have swallowed but her mouth had grown dry.

Determined to keep things light and playful, she crooked a finger his way. "Water's just right. Come on in."

He swung back the shower curtain and stepped over the tub, coming up beside her. In his eyes, she saw passion and fire, a burning in his gaze that had indeed been shadowed by the curtain between them.

He reached out and spanned her waist with his full hands. He might not want possession or ownership, he might not even desire a relationship, but she felt his touch branding her as his own with an imprint that went deeper than her skin. One that couldn't be washed away by the droplets of water pelting her flesh, and one that would last infinitely longer than he'd stay in her life.

"No matter how many times I tell myself to keep my hands off you, I can't do it." His desire-laden voice cut through to her heart.

No time like the present, Grace thought. "Tell me again why you think you should keep your distance."

He laughed. "I don't remember telling you the first time."

She couldn't contain a smile at his ability to catch her each time she attempted to put one over on him. "Then tell me now."

"I can think of better things to do than talk."

She couldn't. She wanted answers and she wanted them now...until he dipped his head and began to lick at the moisture trickling down her neck and shoulders with long, delicious laps of his tongue. She shuddered at the unexpected assault, trembled as he worked his way lower, tasting the water on her chest, following the curve of her breast downward until his tongue lapped relentlessly at her rigid, sensitive nipple.

She felt the sensation of his touch on her breast, her throat and it spread to the spot between her legs, becoming a violent onslaught against all of her senses at one time. His hands cupped her waist tighter, as if he knew she couldn't remain standing without his help. But then she realized he had an ulterior motive because he replaced his tongue with his teeth, grazing at her nipple, pulling the rigid peak into his mouth and suckling so hard her knees buckled.

He turned her around and sat her back against the tub, so she was facing the pelting water that now reflected off his back. He knelt down along with her, nudging her knees apart and settling himself between her legs.

He cupped her tender breast in his hand and held her, gently, almost reverently. "Are you always so responsive?"

Grace leaned her head back against the wall. She'd been with men, thought during those few times she'd been making love. She'd been wrong. She'd had sex.

She and Ben had made love.

Even now, with just foreplay, she was closer to him than she'd ever been to another man. He took her to sexual highs and encouraged her to explore her sensuality, all without directly asking anything from her. Her responsiveness now was in direct correlation to the feelings and emotions tied up with this man.

She met his patient gaze. "Are you looking for an honest answer?"

That seemed to take him by surprise and he jerked backward. "I wouldn't have asked otherwise."

She forced a smile at the disparity between what he was asking and what he was willing to give. "I get it.

I answer honestly, you avoid answering. Not a fair deal, if you ask me."

He shook his head and water flung from the longer strands. "You're a smart cookie. Okay, tell you what. You answer honestly now, and I'll answer your other question later."

She bit down on her lower lip and pondered his offer, knowing he was buying time, and would probably find another excuse to stall later.

His hand plumped her breast, careful to avoid directly stimulating her again, but definitely teasing her all the same.

"I need an answer. Before the water turns cold and forces us out." He punctuated his statement with a revolving motion of his thumb around her distended nipple.

She stifled a gasp, sucked in the combination of pleasure and sensitized pain, and made her decision. "You win. I'll answer." Was she always this responsive? "No, Ben. Never before. No one's ever taken this kind of time or care."

He brushed a damp strand of hair out of her face. "Well, they damn well should have."

She grinned at his ferocious, protective tone. "You're the first man to separate Grace, the woman, from the Montgomery name and money. The first man unrelated to that part of my life who brings out the best in m—" She didn't get a chance to finish. He leaned forward and sealed his lips over hers, cutting off her answer.

Probably because he feared the implications, and as Grace felt the rapid beating of her heart, she knew he was right to avoid hearing the rest.

His kiss was brief but sweet, and she tasted his unique flavor. The beating in her heart became a throbbing of desire between her legs. As if he sensed her need and understood, he stood, swung one leg around her back and lowered himself to a sitting position behind her. Wrapping his arms around her waist, he pulled her against his chest, and into the V of his legs until his penis pushed hard and erect against the small of her back. Water pelted from the showerhead, directly in front of her, hitting by her knees, and keeping them warm.

"Comfortable?" he whispered in her ear.

She nodded. "And curious." A drumming of anticipation thundered in her veins, and his laugh reverberated through her.

"I like your lack of inhibitions."

"Must have something to do with you, because I'd never imagined myself doing anything like...*this.*" Without warning, his hands encircled her thighs and spread them wide. She sucked in a breath. "What are you doing?"

"Trust me, Gracie. Now take a deep breath and let it out. Relax."

Remembering that she'd asked him to trust her earlier, Grace did as he asked, inhaling and exhaling, feeling her body release its hold and let go of its fear. Her muscles slackened against him until she felt his heart beat against her back. A warm and welcoming feeling of security stole over her. *Trust me*, he'd asked. And she did. Much more than she should.

"Better?"

She nodded.

"Okay, ready?"

She leaned her head back against his chest. "For what?"

"Keep leaning against me, sweetheart." He nudged her forward, slowly but insistently, until the warm spray of the shower moved up her legs, from her knees to her thighs and higher. Until the pelting water hit her most sensitive juncture, sluicing over her feminine mound and pummeling at her swollen, moist folds of flesh.

Shock at the intimate assault came first and she instinctively attempted to close her legs but his firm grip stopped her. "Breath deep," his rough, seducing voice murmured again in her ear. "Relax. Enjoy."

With each word, he eased his hold on her thighs and moved his hands inward. A man with an obvious mission, his fingers inched towards *there*, closer, faster, hotter, deeper... Without warning, he parted her flesh and eased one long finger inside. Her hips bucked, drawing him further into her. The roughness of his skin mixed with the water and her own moisture, making for an easy glide in, a slickened slide out. In. Out. Her body echoed the rhythm, picking up a motion of its own that created a surge of need so strong, she had to twist and pull her legs upward to get him deep enough, hard enough inside her.

"Not alone." Grace heard the plea in a voice she barely recognized as her own.

"Condoms are in the living room, and I'm not about to stop you now." He kept up the unbearable friction with his finger, while parting her gently with his other hand. Water crashed down on private, intimate parts she'd never exposed before and the building waves were so incredible, so fast, she could barely keep her sanity. Her body clenched and unclenched around his hand, and climax beckoned, almost there and yet so out of reach.

"Close your eyes."

Had they been open? He couldn't know and neither did she. "Now feel." He pushed deep inside her, hotter, more demanding. "It's me inside you, Gracie. Just me, no condom, nothing to come between us."

She heard the fantasy, she *felt* the fantasy. The final wave rushed her without warning, and she screamed, heard her cries as her body wrung tight around his, clenching, grinding, undulating in never-ending waves of completion.

Only then did she realize she'd been the recipient of his fantasy, but she had yet to indulge in her own.

But the night wasn't over yet.

BEN WRAPPED HER IN A TOWEL and carried her limp, sated body to the bed. She curled close to his chest and rested her head on his shoulder with a satisfied moan.

Had he really thought that by not facing her when she climaxed, he wouldn't be affected? Had he really believed that if he didn't come inside her, he'd remain detached? Hell, had he been stupid enough to buy into the belief that he wasn't falling hard for this woman he was deceiving?

He laid her onto her gingham comforter and propped her up against the pillows, then turned away.

"Where are you going?" Panic tinged her voice, causing guilt and regret to swamp him once more.

"To get myself a towel. I'm dripping all over your floor." Without waiting for her reply, he headed for the steam-filled bathroom, the site of his latest sin, and yanked a towel off a hook behind the door. He dried himself off and grabbed his briefs from the floor in the living room, pulling them on in the futile hope the barrier would provide him with some needed restraint.

When he returned, she was waiting for him just as he'd left her. She gazed at him through heavy-lidded eyes. "Sorry. I didn't mean to panic on you. Can I ask you for something? I know I said I wouldn't, but this...it would mean a lot to me."

"Anything." He spoke without thinking, but wouldn't retract that one word. Instead he lowered himself beside her. The fragrant scent of soap and shampoo lingered in the air, reminding him of their shower, and how she'd come apart in his arms.

Anything, he thought. He wanted to give her anything she desired. "What is it?"

"Stay the night."

At least she wasn't asking for a lifetime. Ben's gut clenched hard. A lifetime, the one thing they could never share, was the one thing he could so easily imagine. He shook himself out of that particular fantasy. "I can manage that."

"Thanks."

"None necessary. But we need to dry you off before we can crawl under the covers." He tugged at the end of the towel he'd wrapped around her and pulled open the ends.

Her skin was red from the heated water and the scratch of his unshaven face, her makeup was long gone, and damp strands of unbrushed hair fell over her cheeks. And still she was the most beautiful woman he'd ever laid eyes upon.

She shivered. "It's cold."

"Then let me warm you." He joined her on the bed and pulled the towel out from beneath her, then he began to pat her legs dry with the fluffy material, working his way upward, starting with her toes.

"You're pampering me," she murmured.

"Yup."

"It's nice."

"Something you're used to?" he asked, wondering just how luxurious her previous life had been.

"Not really, although we grew up in a mausoleum of a house we called *The Estate*, and we had servants galore...but we also had Emma."

The warmth and love in her tone was unmistakable. Having met the impish older woman, Ben could understand Grace's affection. "Your grandmother." He moved from her toes to her ankles, working his way up her skin with slow, circular motions.

"Mmm. Emma kept us grounded. She didn't let us take advantage of the help or use them as our personal maids. Logan and I learned early on to pick up after and take care of ourselves."

He wanted to hear more about her life and deliberately slowed his movements. "You keep talking about Emma and Logan. You never mention the rest of your family. What about your parents?"

She levered herself up, resting her weight on her elbows. "I'm going to answer your questions, because after all we've just shared, I want to open up to you. But make no mistake, the next round is mine."

He laughed. "Okay, go on."

"My parents are my parents in name only. Or should I say especially in name. Nothing's more important to them than the Montgomery name, the legacy, the money—not even their kids. We were expected to be trained pets, taken out for show when it looked good for my father, the judge, to have family around, and ignored the rest of the time."

The pain of her childhood was evident in her voice and by the way she'd clenched her jaw tight. He'd been curious, but he hadn't meant to make her relive unpleasant memories or tense up on him now. "Was it really that bad?"

She nodded. "When I was fifteen I wanted to run for class president. I decided I wasn't going to tell my family until I'd won. It was my way of carrying on the Montgomery family tradition and, let's face it, I desperately wanted to please my father. But it was just another futile attempt to get him to pay attention to me."

"What happened?"

"Someone told him about the race and I came in to school to find he'd spoken to the teachers and volunteered to speak at an assembly on the proper way to handle a campaign. And when Judge Montgomery speaks, people listen."

"Did you win the campaign?"

"Sure did, but not on my own merit. Because my father the judge had convinced every kid present that Montgomerys were born to be public servants and that a vote for Grace was a vote for the constitution."

His gut clenched at the way her father had so obviously belittled her in front of her friends and teachers. At the way she'd spent a lifetime trying to please a man who couldn't be pleased, and how she'd lost herself in the process. But she was on her way back now and he couldn't be more proud of her.

"I'm sure people saw through your father." He knew his words were lame.

"Maybe. But they voted his way anyhow. It was revolting. The other runner-up was so much better qualified. I wanted to run against him and win because I'd swayed people my way. Instead I won on the family name and because my father called in all the favors people owed him. As if I wasn't smart enough to win on my own."

"You must know now you're smarter than any of those kids you went to school with."

She shrugged.

"But I'm sorry you had to live through that. And even sorrier you had to relive it by repeating the story to me now."

She met his gaze with glistening eyes. "Don't be. If I didn't want you to know, I wouldn't have shared. Besides it wasn't all bad. I had Logan and Emma who loved me for myself. And if you ever met my grandmother, you'd understand what a different experience she can be. Eccentric doesn't begin to cover it."

He agreed, not that he was free to tell Grace. "And you adore her."

She nodded.

With the ends of the towel, he traveled a path up the inside of her thighs, until her skin began to quiver and her legs started to shake. "Ben."

Warning tinged her tone and he laughed. "Yes, Gracie."

"I know exactly what you're up to."

"I should hope so."

She let out a near-growl of frustration. "You're avoiding answering questions."

"Untrue. I'm merely taking advantage of your gloriously naked body." He settled himself between her thighs and using the terry towel, he rubbed gently over the damp folds of skin lying bare for his touch.

At his first caress, she moaned softly and his body hardened upon hearing the seductive, husky sound. He rolled over, taking her with him.

Grace knew she'd found heaven in Ben's arms. She'd find answers later. Just feeling the strength of his need pressing against her thigh, and desire bordering on exquisite pain rippled through her. She lifted her hips, thrust herself against him, welcomed the beginning waves. But knowing how incredible making love with Ben was, she didn't want just solitary pleasure, so she raised her head toward the nightstand.

She looked him in the eye, and his gaze deepened, darkened. The next few seconds passed in a rush of anticipation as he shed his briefs and took care of protection. And then he was back, kneeling over her, spreading her legs wider.

"Sit up."

She couldn't ignore the command and pushed herself up on her elbows.

"Now look."

She did, gazing down as he spread her with his fingers, seeing her own dampness beckon to him, and watching as he eased the long, hard length of his erection into her swollen, waiting flesh.

"It's so erotic," she whispered in awe at the sight of

their bodies locked intimately together with the feel of every rigid inch of him filling her. A feast for the senses, she thought, in a daze, unable to distinguish the host of feelings swamping her.

He eased her back down, until he was lying on top of her, moving inside her, *making love to her*. And she refused to believe what they shared was anything less. Especially when every upward thrust not only brought him deeper, but closer to her heart.

9

GRACE WOKE UP WITH A SHIVER and realized she'd rolled away from Ben in the middle of the night. They'd fallen asleep exhausted in each other's arms on top of the covers and when she'd eased away from his body heat, she'd instantly sensed the change.

"You okay?" he asked in a sleep-roughened voice.

"Yeah. Just cold." Better that than to admit she'd missed him. He'd think her ridiculous since he was lying beside her throughout the night. The last thing she wanted to risk was spooking him away.

Though it was dark, the lights from neighboring buildings filtered into the room and Grace could easily make out his masculine form. She shivered again, this time because looking at him made her realize how fortunate she was that he'd come into her life. That a man as caring and sexy as Ben had accepted her. All of her.

"Grace? I asked if you wanted to get beneath the covers."

His voice intruded on her thoughts. "Oh, yes. But there's something I wanted to do first." She swung her legs off the bed and leaned down to retrieve a stack of pictures from beneath the nightstand.

"I take it you're not tired anymore?"

She grinned. "I have lots of stamina. A little rest and I'm raring to go. Unless you'd rather sleep?"

"Sweetheart, I can more than keep up with your stamina. What did you have in mind?"

She snapped on the bedside light and turned back to face him. "Get those naughty thoughts out of your head—at least for now." He'd turned down the covers and she joined him in her bed, pushing away the thought of how lonely it would be for her once he was gone.

"What do you have there?"

She glanced down at the album in her hand, suddenly embarrassed. What had seemed like such a good idea in the dark didn't seem as smart now that the lights were on.

In the dark, she'd thought Ben would like to see the pictures she'd taken in the park. She'd thought that he'd understand what drew her to give something back to these hardworking mothers and their children. That he'd be interested in her and the passion that guided her. But beneath the harsh glare of the lamp's light, Grace saw their situation for what it really was.

It was an affair. A passionate one, to be sure, but a short-term relationship nonetheless. And a man who'd made it clear he wasn't interested in anything that involved commitment wouldn't be interested in what made Grace Montgomery tick.

Even if Grace had stupidly fallen in love with him.

Grace paused in shock. She'd fallen in love with Ben. She clutched the photo album against her chest. "It's nothing important."

He grabbed for her arm and gently swung her around to face him. "I doubt that." He pried her fingers off the plastic binder until he held her life's work in his hands. "These are your pictures," he said without opening the cover.

She managed a nod.

"I can see in your eyes how special these are to you."

"They're a part of me. Proof that I can accomplish what I want to." She shrugged self-consciously. "Kind of silly, huh?"

"You aren't silly. Neither are the things you desire. And that's something I'd like to know—what would those be?"

Passion still simmered in his eyes and found an answer inside her. "Other than you?"

He grinned. "Other than me."

"Did you ever hear of the charity called CHANCES?"

"Vaguely."

"It helps underprivileged children. Remember what I said in the park about giving back? Well, this is how. They've hired me to do the photos and layout for their new brochure and a spread in *Town and Country* magazine. I'm hoping to be able to show the folks back home what real life is like—and collect their cash at the same time." She laughed, feeling embarrassed at her lofty goals.

Admiration shone in his gaze. "I want to see them."

"Well, most are photos of children. I adore children, and capturing them enjoying life, no matter what their background—well, there's nothing better."

"Do you ever think about having kids?"

"Sometimes." She glanced away. The truth was she'd love to have a family, a close-knit, fun family, so unlike her own.

She realized now she wanted that family with Ben. The man who didn't do commitments. She swallowed over the lump in her throat and looked at the photo album again. "Take a look at these." She deliberately changed the subject. "I've given copies of these to the parents for free so they can enjoy their kids, too. So that's it." She gestured to the book. "A broad spectrum of life."

"My mother would understand you so well." He settled in beside her, then ran a hand through his already disheveled hair. "She loved life. Even when things were toughest for us financially, when she worked all day scrubbing other people's floors for a living, she still appreciated the little things. The butterflies in spring and the snowflakes in winter." He patted the space beside him.

Grace crawled back into bed, cuddling next to him. Whether he realized it or not, he'd treated her to a window inside his soul and she'd never take that gift for granted. She placed a hand on his bare arm, knowing he'd chosen this time to open up to her because he sensed how difficult she'd suddenly found it to show him her photos.

And Grace realized that, in her embarrassment, she'd misjudged him. But not entirely, because he wouldn't have the album in his hand now if her gut instinct hadn't trusted him all along.

She intended to make sure he never regretted letting her in. "And now your mother can't see the things she loves."

He shook his head. "Only shadows."

If she hadn't been looking, she'd have missed the flash of pain and regret that crossed his face.

"Ben, you need to remember life goes on for her in other ways. The things she keeps with her in here." She tapped her chest, near her heart. "And here." She pointed to her head. "Even if she never sees a sunset again, the memory will sustain her."

His gaze locked with hers. Surprise registered first, then gratitude flickered in his eyes. "I should have known you'd understand."

She reached for his hand. "I'm not sure why you thought I wouldn't. While we're on the subject of your mother, what happened to your father? I've never heard you mention him."

"He was a good man. He died when I was eight. Heart attack," he added, answering her unasked question.

"I'm sorry. And here I was complaining about my parents ignoring me. At least both of mine were there."

A scowl creased his forehead. "Don't apologize for being unhappy with the hand you were dealt. A child has a right to expect love and concern from their parents." He squeezed her hand back and she realized they weren't only sharing stories, they were sharing comfort. And it felt good.

It had been too long since she'd had someone to just hold on to. When she was young, she'd always had Logan to comfort her when things got rough at home. Her poor brother had spent too many late nights massaging her forehead to alleviate pounding migraines thanks to the incessant arguments between her parents. The ones behind the walls, the ones they didn't think anyone could hear. Because Montgomerys didn't argue in public where everything was picture-perfect. But Grace had grown up and she hadn't had anyone to lean on for too long.

Now she had Ben. She rested her head on his shoulder and warned herself not to get used to it, but her heart, beating hard against her chest, refused to face the truth right now. Until he walked out, he was hers.

"I'm not saying I had a perfect life, but you must think I'm pretty ridiculous. Talking about mansions and Porsches, servants and money while complaining in the same breath." She paused and let out a long sigh. "As clichéd as it sounds, though, money can't buy happiness."

"I don't think you're ridiculous. I think you've had a long road toward growing up. But you've gotten there and you should be proud." He paused. "And to think all the years I thought I had it rough...looks like I was lucky." He flipped open the album cover, exposing her pictures to the light of day.

But embarrassment around Ben was no longer an issue, and as he perused her collection, Grace wasn't worried about what he'd think or whether he'd approve.

She already knew. With Ben occupied, she pondered this last conversation and the realization sunk in. He both liked and respected her. All of her, no secrets, no hiding, everything laid out for him to see. And he hadn't belittled her. He'd praised her instead.

"What you just said? That means more than you'll ever know," she whispered.

Ben knew—more than he should about Grace and what made her tick. Not only what turned her on, but what motivated her actions. Looking at the pictures from the park—the children on the swings being pushed by their fathers, the kids with ice cream dripping down their faces and into a puddle on the floor and finally the mothers holding crying infants in their arms—Ben knew Grace was as traditional, sweet and guileless as they came.

She wanted everything she'd been denied growing up. The loving family. He'd even go so far as to say she desired the white picket fence, the 2.5 kids and the dog. And damned if he couldn't imagine her with all of that and more.

But in the meantime, she was trying to make up for having so much wealth when others did not. She wasn't handing out money, but something far more precious. She was giving these hardworking people memories to cherish. The kind of loving memories she'd never had.

"Today's Sunday." Grace's soft voice cut into Ben's thoughts. "Will you be visiting your mother today?"

He met her clear-eyed gaze. "Yeah. Around four. I usually stay for dinner." And damned if he didn't want to bring her with him. But he wouldn't. He'd only be setting Grace up for disappointment and pain later if he allowed her deeper into his personal life.

And there was his mother to consider—his feisty mother who wanted to see him married and had even resorted to pumping her elderly neighbors for information about their single daughters. No way could Ben bring a woman around. Her sight was gone, not her mind. She'd draw the right conclusions about Grace, and then Ben would have to explain why he'd had to let her go—and suffer a motherly lecture on his improper behavior.

He glanced down at a photo of a bright, sunny day, the park aglow with the faces of happy children. No hint of poverty or disillusionment in sight. "Amazing how different the park looks through your eyes."

He met her gaze. Her face had flushed pink and she beamed with pride in her work. He looked back down and turned the next page. The setting had changed to shadows instead of sunlight, an alley instead of the park. "Like the picnics my mother took me on. I'd forget all the bad things that ever happened to us."

Ben felt the same peace and contentment around Grace. Uncomfortable with the thought, he glanced down. She had focused in on one child with her zoom lens. She'd captured a wide-eyed imp waving for the camera with an obvious look of glee on his face, as if she'd caught him being naughty and enjoying it.

But it was the flash of red in the background that caught Ben's attention. He gently pried the photo out of its holder.

"What are you doing?" she asked.

"Getting a closer look." He held the picture up to the light and squinted. "If I didn't know better..."

"What is it?" She sat up behind him and rested against his back so she could look over his shoulder. Her bare breasts brushed against his skin. Only then did he realize they'd been sitting nude, discussing their lives, sharing their pasts in a purely comfortable state. Like he'd caught his parents doing one morning when he'd stumbled into their bedroom without knocking. Like an old married couple.

"Well? What is it?" she asked.

He forced himself to refocus on the picture. "The guy that attacked you if I'm not mistaken. When was this taken?"

"Same day."

"Same red cutoff shirt. It was the first thing I noticed after I heard you scream. The flash of red." He squinted again. "Take a look at what's in his hands."

She leaned closer. All he had to do was turn around and she'd be in his arms.

"It's hard to see. I followed Kurt—the little boy—from the playground. He disappeared when his mother wasn't looking. He's good at that—always going after his big brother."

"Ever meet the brother?"

"No. He makes himself scarce. From what his mother tells me, he does the same thing at school. Anyway, I followed Kurt to a back alley. He turned, saw me behind him and knew he'd been caught. He knew I'd drag him back to his mother, but the look on his face was priceless, so I snapped the picture."

"And you caught a lot more than a precocious kid. Looks like a bag of white powder in your attacker's hand."

"Give me that." She grabbed the picture. "I can't make that out. How can you?"

Gut instinct, Ben thought. He'd seen similar situations going down too many times in his younger days. Hell, he'd been lucky he hadn't gotten caught up in it himself. But taking care of his mother had always come first. "I told you I grew up in a neighborhood like this. That picture is trouble."

"So that explains the note," she whispered.

He stiffened. "What note?"

She exhaled and bent down, pulling a crumpled sheet of paper from the bedside garbage. "This one."

After handing him the letter, she cuddled up behind him and pressed a kiss to his neck. He shivered against her heated touch. "Stop trying to distract me, Gracie. When'd you get this?"

She sighed. "This afternoon. Kurt handed it to me while I was sitting at the playground. Innocent as can be."

He muttered a curse that was modified for her benefit. "And you still took the subway back tonight?"

"If you'll calm down and remember, I never left the sidewalk outside the entrance. I just did a complete circle—and I knew you were behind me the whole time. I was safe."

He appreciated the vote of confidence but not her cavalier attitude. "Do you have any idea what this means?" He waved the photo in the air.

She sat back. "That Kurt's big brother is into drugs and Kurt's seen way too much for a boy his age."

"That, too. But it also means you caught something illegal on film. They know it or they don't want to risk the chance that you might get something in the future. Either way you're a walking target."

Grace shivered at his deliberately blunt words.

He turned and held her close. "I don't want you scared, I just want you careful."

Her soft hands snaked around his waist. "Well, how about I'll be both? Because my pictures have to get taken. So I guess it's a good thing I have you for backup."

"I distinctly remember you dismissing the need out of hand."

"I'm independent, not stupid. I also know my limitations. Tripping him won't take care of the problem."

He knew what a huge concession he'd just been given. Grace had worked too hard to become her own person. She wouldn't admit her need for help easily. Hell, she'd fought his attempts to watch out for her often enough in the past week.

He pulled out of her embrace. "Know what I like about you?"

"What's that?" Her eyes sparkled with curiosity.

"You're a smart woman."

"Because I admit I need you?"

He shook his head. It wasn't that simple. "Because you're willing to compromise your hard-won independence until we resolve this. First thing tomorrow, I'll go on down and ask some questions while you're at work. Hopefully by the time you get there for lunch, I'll have some answers."

"You knew I'd be going anyway?"

"I know *you.*"

"And you aren't going to try to talk me out of it?"

He shrugged. "Would it do any good?"

She laughed. "Not a bit."

He'd known that. "Which is why the best I can do is be there first, to stake things out and keep an eye on you. Leon—the guy from the basketball courts—has a lot of connections. I'll discover something. Find some way to make it safe for you down there.

What had begun as a search for information for her grandmother had just turned into something far more personal: his personal crusade to keep Grace safe.

Her hands came to rest on his chest, her flat palms covering his nipples. He let out a strangled groan. "Grace, this is serious."

"I know. And my private detective and his expertise will take care of the threat. In the meantime, I'm going to take care of you."

A PERSISTENT RINGING WOKE Ben out of a sound sleep. Surrounded by warmth—Gracie's warmth—he had no desire to move. A steady knocking began to accompany the doorbell's harsh sound.

Beside him, Grace groaned. "Go away."

"Not a morning person?" Leaning over, he brushed her hair off her face and placed a kiss on her cheek. "That's okay. I liked your kind of night games." He sat up and swung his legs over the side of the bed.

She didn't answer, not even a playful response or swat.

He chuckled, realizing he even liked her grumpy and disheveled in the morning. He pulled on his jeans, standing to zip them, but not taking the time to button the fly. "Sure you want me to get that?" Because he had no desire to answer her door half-dressed. "The neighbors might talk."

She yanked the pillow over her head in response.

He laughed all the way to the door...until he glanced out the peephole. Standing in the hall were two well-dressed, good-looking people, people he'd seen in photographs around Grace's apartment. The man studied his watch in concern while the woman patted his arm and tried knocking again.

If Ben had hesitated about answering her door before, he really didn't like doing it now. He glanced back toward the bedroom.

"Come on, Grace," the male voice in the hall called out.

Ben groaned. He had no choice.

"Doorman said you're here. It's...your brother," Logan said, just as Ben swung the door open wide. "You're not my sister." The concern on Logan's features turned into an open scowl as his gaze swept Ben, from his morning razor stubble, to his unbuttoned jeans, to his bare feet.

Ben liked the situation even less now. He didn't have any siblings, but he knew without a doubt, if he were in Logan's place, he'd want to kill. No matter that his sister was an adult, this first, and only, meeting would not go smoothly.

"Well, this is awkward." A blond woman wearing black jeans, a black T-shirt and a wide, leopard-print headband stepped forward. "I'm Catherine, Grace's sister-in-law. And this is her brother, Logan."

She jabbed her husband in the ribs. "Quit scowling. Grace is an adult. She's entitled to live her life the same way we are. Don't jump all over her the second you see her and give her even more reason to back off."

Catherine paused in her monologue to stick her hand out toward Ben. "And you are...?"

He grinned. Yet another member of this family he liked immediately. "Ben Callahan. Neighbor." He figured bare minimum information was sufficient. Unfortunately the details were all too obvious.

After shaking Catherine's hand, Ben extended his hand to Logan. He understood the other man's glaring silence but he wouldn't be rude to people Grace cared about.

The man accepted the gesture. "Doesn't mean I approve," he muttered.

"Good thing I don't need your permission then." Grace's voice sounded from behind Ben.

He turned in time to see her, a blur in floor-length blue terry robe, squeal in delight and run past him, first to Logan and then to Catherine, enclosing them both in a loving embrace. The sight caused a lump in Ben's throat because it showed him how much she loved—and was loved—by her family. And how much she was missing by living alone in New York. And, also, how right he was about her returning to the life she'd left behind. One day soon. Even if she didn't realize it yet.

Ben had been given this one night. The glaring light of day had come too soon.

"What are you doing here?" Grace asked her brother.

"Do you think you can be silent for so long and not have me check up on you?"

She shrugged. "Sorry. But I'm still glad you're here."

"Besides," Catherine added, "we wouldn't miss your birthday."

"Birthday?" Ben spoke without thinking.

"Yes, birthday. Tomorrow." Logan raised an unamused eyebrow and Ben could practically hear his unspoken thought. *You slept with my sister and you don't even know her birthday's tomorrow? Just how well do you really know my sister?*

Too well, Ben thought. Too damn well, and a small detail like not knowing her birthday couldn't change what had happened between them. But he knew when to make an exit, and the pounding in his chest and the sheen of sweat on his forehead told him now was the opportune moment.

While Grace brought her family into the apartment, Ben ducked into the bedroom and finished dressing. He refused to think, to deal with his emotions or anything else until he got the hell out of there.

He walked out of the bedroom to find them all sitting in the living room. The room was still littered with candles, though the sensual goodies they'd never gotten to had been moved—and Ben was grateful Grace had swept them away. And though neither Logan nor Grace had commented on the seductive atmosphere, it wasn't something that could be missed.

"Ben, come get to know Cat and Logan. If you're lucky, they'll even tell you the story of how they got together. My grandmother handpicked Cat, then set them up and locked them in a closet together in the middle of a party."

"Your grandmother sounds like a real character," Ben said.

"You don't know the half of it. Her matchmaking shenanigans put the most seasoned pro to shame." Catherine shook her head and chuckled. "I can laugh about it. *Now.*"

Grace patted the couch beside her. "Have a seat. Logan's finished with the protective older brother routine." Logan still scowled, but Grace seemed, or pretended, not to notice. Her gentle laugh floated around the room and squeezed Ben's heart tight.

He'd miss that sound most of all. "I really need to get going." He wondered if the excuse sounded as lame as he knew it to be.

"No, you don't. Not till four. How about I get dressed, run down and pick up breakfast?" Grace asked.

He inhaled deep. Denying her anything was damn difficult. "How about I run down and pick up breakfast? You visit with your family."

Her face lit up and she nodded. Ben knew she

thought he'd be staying to eat with them. But he wouldn't.

He slammed the door to the apartment behind him. He'd entered Grace's life based on a lie. He'd also slept with her knowing he was deceiving her, and in an hour, he'd be reporting news of her life back to her grandmother. He had no business socializing with her family like he was a good friend or something more. Grace certainly wouldn't appreciate the truth if she knew it—and neither would her brother.

"So where's the baby?" Grace asked her brother, minutes after Ben's abrupt departure.

"Home with Emma, and stop changing the subject. Who's the guy?"

"Would you leave her alone?" Catherine complained, siding with Grace in a gesture of female unity.

Logan gave his wife a pointed look. "Did *you* back off your sister, Kayla, when she started with Kane?"

Grace curled her feet beneath her, enjoying the familial argument, the loving bickering between her brother and his wife. She'd missed them terribly and was grateful they'd come to visit. She just wished their timing had been better. The way Ben had hightailed it out of here after dropping off breakfast, Grace knew their intrusion had destroyed the warmth and intimacy of their night together.

He'd backed off again and, this time, it wouldn't be as easy to bring him back.

After a too-short visit, Grace dropped Logan and

Catherine at a hotel. Catherine was operating on sleep deprivation thanks to her teething baby and needed a nap before heading home. She'd claimed she didn't want to displace Grace and take her bed, but Grace sensed Logan and Cat needed time alone.

Grace was left on her own, feeling restless and jittery. Adrenaline from her night with Ben floated through her veins, and with a long day stretching ahead of her, Grace couldn't sit still. Besides she had to have a talk with little Kurt's mother before the child followed in his big brother's footsteps, if he hadn't already. Grace didn't know exactly what his brother was into or how deep, but she couldn't worry about getting him into trouble. Nor could she worry about her own personal safety. Not when a still innocent boy's life was at stake.

Grabbing her camera, Grace headed downtown.

10

THE PHONE RANG THE MOMENT Ben walked into his apartment. Visiting his mother had lifted his spirits—how could it not when nothing got the older woman down? The harsh ring sounded once more. Knowing it was probably Emma threatened his improved mood, but why put off the inevitable?

He grabbed for the receiver. "Callahan."

"Good afternoon!" Emma's cheery voice came through the line loud and too clear.

"Hi, Emma." He deliberately omitted any sentence with *good* in the equation.

"Late night last night?"

"I take it you tried calling this morning?"

"Why, yes. I wanted to warn you Grace's brother was coming for a surprise visit but I assume you found out the hard way?"

"Excuse me?"

Ben nearly choked with guilt. The older woman couldn't possibly have known anything was going on between himself and Grace. If she did, she'd kick him off the case and out of this apartment so fast his head would spin. Of course since Logan now knew of Ben's overnight activities, there was a good chance

Emma would, too. Unless Logan wanted to protect his grandmother's delicate sensibilities and had remained silent. Ben swallowed a laugh. There wasn't one thing delicate about Emma's sensibilities—if she even had any.

"I've been calling since nine. Not home last night, not home first thing this morning, out all afternoon. You've been busy. So you know Logan and Cat have made an appearance...because you're watching Grace's every move, I mean."

"Of course." He shook his head. "I mean, yes, I know your grandson is here."

If nothing else, Ben had felt free to visit his mother knowing Logan and Cat would keep Grace busy for the day. He hadn't had to worry about Grace making a solo trip to the park or getting into another tangle with Kurt's big brother.

"Logan's a wonderful man," Emma mused. "Took a little doing to get him together with Catherine, but I was up to the challenge."

"Of course you were." Why did Ben suspect Logan Montgomery would have had an easier time getting together with Catherine if the older woman had stayed out of things instead?

"And Grace?"

His gut clenched at the sound of her name. With need. With longing. With more guilt than he could have imagined just days earlier, when he'd taken the case.

He had no desire to reveal any information about

Grace's life to her grandmother. His client. The person to whom he owed his loyalty. He didn't want to inform Emma that Grace had friends from all walks of life or that she had a decent job taking pictures for a charity brochure, a job that was a stepping stone to bigger and better things. He didn't even want to reveal that she was happy. Anything and everything felt like a betrayal of the worst kind.

But he'd already accepted money for expenses on this assignment, already lived in an apartment Emma paid rent on, already put his mother on a waiting list for the next available space in the assisted living facility of her choice—a place where she could remain among friends and retain as much quality of life as possible.

On a professional level, he'd promised Emma his best. On a personal level, he'd promised his mother even more. He owed them both. Refusing to think about where that placed Grace in the scheme of his life, he refocused on the conversation with her grandmother.

"I'm nearly done here. I have all the information you need to rest easy where your granddaughter is concerned. I just need another day or two to wrap things up on my end."

To check out the attacker at the park, and to let the police in on the other guy's extra-curricular activities. Once Ben knew the cops were watching the attacker, and the neighborhood kids who lived on the courts were keeping an eye on Grace in the meantime, Ben's job here would be finished. "I'll let you know when I'm ready to move on and I'll send you a formal report."

Emma made what sounded like a choking sound and began to cough heavily into the phone.

"Are you okay?" he asked.

"Yes." A few seconds of silence followed, then Ben heard what sounded like water being swallowed. "Sorry. What I was trying to say was I'm impressed with how fast you work."

He thought of Grace lying naked beneath him. The older lady didn't know the half of it. "Thank you," he somehow managed to answer.

"I don't need a written report. Your word is fine with me."

"I appreciate that, but it's how I always close a case." And that's what Ben was hoping for this time, too.

Closure that wasn't too painful.

"Well, I enjoyed working with you and I'll look forward to seeing for myself. I mean, reading for myself. Bye."

He replaced the receiver and began straightening the place as best he could. But his gaze kept straying to the door, as if he could see what was going on across the hall. He was torn by the desire to see Grace again and the knowledge that getting to know her family would only make his leaving more difficult.

The telephone rang once more. He grabbed the receiver. "I thought we were finished."

"Wrong person, man."

"Hey, Leon." Ben listened to the reason for Leon's call and muttered a curse.

Guilt took on a whole new meaning. He should have known better than to think Grace would trust him to take care of things downtown. That damn independent streak of hers would be the death of him yet...especially if something had happened to her.

He slammed down the phone and took off running.

WHEN BEN ARRIVED, HE FOUND the scene Leon had called him about—an unfamiliar building and a swarm of people with a police car out front. If the subway hadn't been ninety degrees he would have broken into a sweat from fear alone—until he caught sight of Grace, unhurt and unharmed. But only because he hadn't gotten hold of her yet.

"Hey, man."

Ben turned toward the tall, lanky kid who excelled on the courts and whom he now owed his unending gratitude. "What happened?"

"Your lady knows how to get into trouble. She shows up with the camera around her neck, snooping around askin' questions like anyone seen Bobby when everyone knows Bobby don't want to be seen. So she takes the little brother out for a walk when everyone knows Bobby's got Kurt running errands for him, if you know what I mean."

"Apparently not everyone knew better than to stay away from Bobby." Ben muttered a curse.

"You got that right." Leon nodded in agreement. "So like I was sayin', she gets herself alone with Kurt and then Bobby gets himself alone with your lady."

Ben's stomach twisted in tight knots. "What happened?"

"Lucky for everyone, Mrs. Ramone knows her boy and she called the cops."

"Before anyone got hurt."

Leon nodded again. "And before anyone sees me ratting I'm outta here."

"You be at the courts tomorrow," Ben called after the youth.

Then he turned toward Grace. The crowd had dispersed and the police were getting into their cars and driving away as Ben made his way to the front stoop of the old building.

He knew better than to lecture Grace in public, but heaven help her when he got her alone. "Hi, Gracie." He clenched his hands into fists at his side.

"Ben!" She stood quickly. "What are you doing... Never mind." She was obviously surprised to see him—and just as obviously aware of his mood because she backed up a step and ended up falling back down on her behind.

She donned a sheepish grin, one he'd have a hard time resisting if fear for her safety wasn't still pumping through his veins.

"Have you ever met Mrs. Ramone? She's Kurt's mother. You remember Kurt? The cute kid in the picture I showed you?"

"I remember the picture," he said through clenched teeth. "Nice to meet you, Mrs. Ramone." Ben shook the older woman's hand, taking in her tearstained face and the weariness in her eyes that made her old before her time.

In Mrs. Ramone, Ben saw all he'd feared happening to his mother, but thanks to her optimism and Ben's determination to get them both out of the old neighborhood fast and safe, Ben's mother had fared much better. Even with the onset of blindness and age, she appeared happier and more youthful than this woman ever had a chance of being.

As he listened, she explained how Grace had shown up at her door, the incriminating photo in hand. She'd sat the woman down and shown her proof that her older son was dealing drugs and her younger son's idolization of his brother would get him in serious trouble. Then she'd taken Kurt for ice cream. On the walk home, she'd run into trouble, in the name of Bobby Ramone.

"But the police were waiting and I'd given them the picture. They have Bobby in custody and we can only hope it's not too late for Kurt," Grace chimed in. "There's an after-school program I've heard about and if we can keep him busy and educated, maybe he won't end up like his brother." Grace rambled, her residual fear still obvious, and her nervousness about letting Ben get a word in equally apparent.

Considering he'd like to throttle her for taking this on alone, he didn't blame her. But he'd learned something else, too. Grace had a big heart—and he loved her for it.

He loved her. And there was no way he could walk away when this case was over.

He glanced at her wide-eyed, apprehensive expression, and though he still wanted to shake her for taking such a huge risk, more than that he wanted to pull her into his arms and *feel* she was safe. Then he could tell her how proud she made him, even as his heart thudded in his chest out of fear for her safety.

But he'd do none of those things. Because he had no right to call Grace Montgomery his. Not when everything between them was based on one huge lie—*his* lie. One only he could correct.

And he would correct it. He had to if he wanted even a chance at a future, and suddenly Ben the loner wanted just that.

Knowing he couldn't deal with Grace, not while the lump in his throat was so huge it threatened to choke him, Ben turned toward Kurt's mother. "If you need anything, you call me."

He stuck his hand into his pocket and retrieved his wallet and business card within. His cases might center on the more privileged because the financial gain was better, but he always helped out friends in the old neighborhood, the one so similar to this one.

"I've got some connections with social services that can help you out, and if your son gets out of jail and wants to go straight, let him get in touch. I'll put him to work and keep an eye on him."

The older woman grabbed him in a bear hug. He inhaled and smelled a combination of musty aromas from the old apartments and the scent of good old-fashioned cooking—all as familiar to him as his own mother. The memories weren't painful any longer, they just *were*. And Ben sensed he had Grace to thank for that. For understanding him. For reaching out and accepting the person he'd once been.

He extended his hand to Grace. "Ready to go?"

Looking wary, she placed a hand in his and allowed him to pull her to a standing position.

"If you're planning on yelling you should know I have sensitive ears," she warned him.

He laughed, though he felt anything but light-hearted. "You've got plenty of sensitive parts," he murmured for her ears only. "I wouldn't expect your ears to be any different. But make no mistake, you are going to hear what I have to say."

She rolled her eyes, but remained silent.

He hoped she understood he intended to have his lecture. She hadn't given him a say in her safety, opting instead to exert that blasted independence of hers. He definitely wasn't through with her yet.

"THEY CAUGHT BOBBY RAMONE with cocaine. Between drug possession and trafficking charges he should be out of commission for a while." Grace glanced at Ben.

His jaw was still clenched tight. He hadn't said a word the entire hot, steamy subway ride and now with their building in sight, she hoped to smooth things over before they went their separate ways. She held no illusions he hadn't gotten over her brother's intrusion and his withdrawal had begun once more.

And obviously he was too furious to deal with her now. Not in the intimate way she desired. A way that would soothe her fears and make her feel safe.

"Don't kid yourself about Bobby," Ben said, breaking the silence. "If he snitches and give the cops bigger fish, he's back on the street and you're back where you started." Ben's mood couldn't have been more grim.

"If you'd been around I'd have let you know I was headed for the park." She crossed her fingers behind her back.

No need for him to know she'd needed to take care of this on her own. No matter how hard her heart had been pounding, no matter how scared she'd been, Grace had to solve this on her own. As much to prove to herself that she was capable of taking care of herself as to know she was capable of making a difference in someone's life. Without the Montgomery name or money. Without Ben's help.

"Don't lie to me." Her hand still held firmly in his, he led her into the building. "And don't kid yourself that this is over—until I've checked it out and know for sure."

Because she sensed his need to be in control and understood, Grace agreed. "Okay."

Silence surrounded them the entire elevator ride

and Grace couldn't think of a way to make amends until he decided to calm down.

Fear still pounded inside Ben when he thought of how badly Grace could have been hurt. Until he'd leashed the adrenaline pumping through his system, he had nothing more to say. He rounded the corner leading to her apartment and stopped short.

A stranger stood in front of Grace's door, suitcase in hand and a stereo-box and folding table leaning against the wall.

"Marcus!" Grace said, a mixture of shock and delight evident in her tone. She rushed forward to give the other man a too-friendly squeeze.

"Don't tell me you've forgotten your grand-mother's annual birthday surprise." The man sounded mockingly offended.

Ben cleared his throat. "And what surprise would that be?" Ben asked.

The other man turned and extended his hand. "Marcus Taylor, Master Masseur at your service."

Masseur. An intrusion he didn't need, but Ben shook Marcus's hand, certain of one thing—he couldn't stand the thought of this man touching Grace. Ben didn't give a damn if the guy made a living with those hands or how professional the contact. He wasn't sliding his fingers down Grace's smooth skin. He wouldn't be the one to make her muscles slacken or elicit those contented sighs.

Ben shook the man's hand then dug into his pocket. "How much are you getting paid for this gig?"

"Ben!" Grace sounded outraged, in her best, snooty Montgomery voice.

He loved it.

Over her protest, Marcus named a sum only Emma Montgomery would pay for an hour's worth of work. "Up front," the man added.

"Tell you what," Ben counted out the money he'd withdrawn earlier today, "the lady and I want to be alone. This ought to cover the use of your equipment, plus some. Take the night off. I'll leave your equipment for you with the doorman."

Grace watched the exchange—of dialogue and cash—mouth open wide. He touched the bottom of her chin and pushed her jaw closed. She stood, arms crossed, eyes huge, but not a word of protest crossed her lips. Ben gained a perverse sense of satisfaction knowing she preferred his touch to the professional's.

"Grace?" Marcus turned toward her.

As additional incentive, Ben added the last hundred-dollar bill in his pocket to the stash. Marcus snatched up the wad of cash Ben had flashed his way. "It'll help pay for the engagement ring my girlfriend's been eyeing," he explained sheepishly.

"At least it's going for something worthwhile," Ben said. Because he sure as hell couldn't afford the expense of paying Marcus off.

He glanced at Grace. Her warm brown eyes had darkened with pleasure and she laughed, a sparkling, infectious laugh. He still had his point to make, but there were more effective ways than yelling, he thought wryly. And as far as his wallet was concerned, some sacrifices were worth the price.

BEN HAD BANISHED HER FROM the bedroom while he set up. Grace paced the floor of her living room, anticipation and desire building inside her. She had no illusions. He was still furious, but at least he'd been jealous over Marcus—jealous enough to buy the man off.

She shivered, knowing as much as she loved her newfound independence, she loved Ben's take charge attitude, too. Especially when he directed it at her.

She waited as he took over her birthday surprise, unable to believe she'd forgotten Emma's ritual. Every year since Grace had turned eighteen, Emma had sent a personal masseur to her granddaughter as a special gift. *Take care of the body and the spirit will follow.* Because Grace had suffered migraines since she was a child, usually brought on by the stress of living under her parents' rigid rules and incessant fights, Emma had insisted she follow that particular prescription for healing. What had begun as a kind of therapy had turned into a birthday gift Grace truly enjoyed—and normally looked forward to.

During the years when she'd lived off her trust, a massage by Marcus had been a weekly event included in her budget. But she was older and wiser these days, and such a frivolity wasn't something she needed. And she realized, now that she wasn't splurging on herself, Emma's gift meant so much more.

So did Ben's.

"Come on in," Ben called out. "Sheet's on the bed. Change and I'll be right out."

A delicious tingling arose inside her as she walked into her room. He'd closed himself in her bathroom, giving her privacy, as Marcus would have done.

She undressed, ignoring the sudden chill on her skin. She'd be warm soon enough. A tremor of awareness shot down her spine, an anticipation unlike any she'd ever felt before. Because this wouldn't be just any massage.

Wrapping herself in the cool sheet, she climbed onto the padded table and stretched out on her stomach, adjusting the sheet until it covered her back, but could be easily removed. "All set," she called out, then rested her head against her arms and waited.

The bathroom door opened. The sound of creaking hinges sounded unnaturally loud in her small bedroom, so did the padded footsteps that came up behind her. "Music?" Ben asked.

"Mmm. The waterfall." Nothing soothed her more than the echo of cascading water and the soft strains of a violin in the background.

He shuffled through the cassettes and placed her choice into the box, then drew the shades and dimmed the lights. The result was a shift in atmosphere. The bubbling sounds of water mentally transported her from her bedroom to a solitary outdoor spot.

Soon, the intoxicating scent of coconut oil filled her nostrils, reminding her of days at the beach and the sinful delights she knew Ben had in store. With each silent minute that passed, her anticipation built. Lying face down, her breasts pressed against the table and a heavy feeling growing between her legs, a need for Ben's touch became overwhelming.

Finally his large, warm hands began their job, working with deep, circular motions against the soles of her feet, relaxing muscles she didn't know she had. Tension and stress seeped out of her body as she was lulled into a blissful state of oblivion.

His firm touch eased its way up her calves and lingered before reaching her thighs—and that's where oblivion ended and awareness took over. Sensual, sexual, heated awareness of the firm touch on the back of her legs and the long fingers easing their way upward, to places no regular masseur would ever venture to go.

"I'm not sure this is within the definition of massage."

"I thought we'd bend the rules a bit." His finger slipped into the moist crevice between her legs and she let out a soft moan. "Considering tomorrow's your birthday and all."

He leaned closer, so his warm breath fanned her neck and his lips brushed the shell of her ear. "Unless you have any objection."

"I already told you I've been a good girl way too long." She paused a beat, letting her words hover between them.

He moved his hand, letting his finger slide provocatively along her wet heat before removing his touch completely. Her body felt the loss and she shuddered, bucking against the table in frustration.

"Easy." His husky reassurance set her nerve endings on fire.

She glanced over in time to see him slicken his fingertips with oil once more. He met her gaze, his eyes dark and glittering with passion. Was it her imagination or did she see an edge to his gaze, a desperation she didn't want to accept?

She knew he hadn't planned anything intimate. In fact, since her brother's arrival, he'd probably planned to back off. *This* interlude was probably his way of letting go of the tension he'd felt earlier when she'd been in danger. She knew her own burning need was to a great extent a release of fear and adrenaline. Of course, for her it was also driven by her love for him and her desire to be loved by him in return.

His hand returned with a smooth glide along her skin, over her buttocks, and dipping into unexplored territory. An unexpected jolt of pleasure shot through her and satisfaction gleamed in his eyes. She shivered and groaned, realizing he wasn't through arousing her in this way any more than she was finished exploring her feminine side and pushing the boundaries of passion.

In both her heart and the depth of her soul, Grace accepted that Ben was the only man she'd ever trust in this intimate way. So if it was desperation she saw in his gaze, she understood because she felt an extreme need to make the most of the time they had left—time, she suddenly realized, that he had granted them.

The knowledge made her brazen enough to give him everything she had and more. So when he walked out of her life, he would never forget Grace Montgomery.

Grace looked at him with greedy eyes, devouring him with her gaze. "I've only been bad with you." A seductive smile curved her lips.

He eased his fingers deeper inside her, moving downward with a glide made easy by the oil and her own feminine dampness. "How's this?"

She trembled beneath his hand. "Not bad, but you can do better."

11

"YOU'RE RIGHT. I CAN." Ben slipped his hands beneath her, lifting her into his arms. He walked around the table, which wouldn't hold their combined weight, and lay her face down on the bed. "Since I didn't know it was your birthday until this morning, I didn't have time to prepare. I don't want you to be disappointed." His heart hammered hard in his chest.

She rolled over and he let her, waiting until she was comfortable to straddle himself over her.

By all rights their time together should be coming to an end but he refused to give her up without a fight. There was nothing he could do about his predicament now, but first thing tomorrow he'd attempt to dig himself out of this mess of lies.

For the time being, he would lose himself inside her and hope she'd forgive him. And hope they'd have a future.

"You could never disappoint me, Ben."

If she only knew how untrue that statement was. He deliberately forced his lies out of his mind.

Her large brown eyes met his. Filled with need and

emotion, she held his stare and wouldn't let go. "I don't want gifts. I just want you."

"Then we're on the same wavelength, sweetheart." Because what he had for Grace wasn't an item to be opened, rather it was a gift from the heart. "But I need your cooperation. And I need your trust."

"You have it." She spoke without hesitation.

That easy, Ben thought. And that complicated. He was about to show her what it felt like to lose control—the same way she made him lose his.

He leaned forward to brush a kiss over her lips and her hands grasped his neck, holding him close. "Uh-uh." He untangled her arms and placed them at her sides.

The gleam in her eyes held more curiosity than anything else. Ben adjusted the sheet that had remained twisted around her until the opening parted in front. Slowly he eased the ends apart, revealing her breasts to his hungry gaze.

He wanted her writhing, begging and pleading for release and then he wanted to watch her explode as he entered her, with his name on her lips. He wanted this to be a birthday she'd never forget.

He laved one nipple with his tongue, dampening the rigid tip and encircling the plump flesh surrounding it. She smelled so damn good and tasted even better. Only focusing on *her* pleasure enabled him to control his own and he paused to blow a stream of cool air over the flesh he'd just bathed.

A strangled sound came from deep inside her,

making him hard with wanting, and then her hand came to rest on his neck and pulled him closer, telling him without words what she needed.

"You've forced my hand, sweetheart."

"How so?" Her voice was rough with desire.

"I can't have those hands of yours distracting me and it's time you learned what it feels like to feel helpless—the way I felt when you ran off today."

She'd taken years off his life and he'd rather cut off his own arm than have anything happen to her. The only reason he hadn't confronted her yet was the unexpected birthday celebration.

He reached for and opened the night table drawer and retrieved the bandannas he'd placed there earlier.

Her eyes widened, but she didn't argue. In fact, she seemed to be enjoying every minute. He lifted one of her wrists and massaged her soft flesh in his hands. "I want you to be okay with this."

Her dark eyes met his. There was that implicit trust again. "There's nothing you can do I'm not okay with."

He could almost see himself through her eyes and wished he could be everything she believed him to be. He looped a scarf around one brass bar on the headboard, then secured her wrist, before doing the same to her other hand. "Comfortable?"

"Aroused," she murmured.

"That's the point." And he knew the feeling. Before

Grace, he'd never known sweatpants could be too damn tight.

Grace looked into Ben's eyes and knew she was telling him the truth. There wasn't another human being she trusted as much as she trusted him to take care of her, body, heart and soul. With her hands tied loosely above her, she was more exposed to him than she'd ever thought she'd allow herself to be to anyone. More vulnerable. And more receptive to anything he desired.

But she couldn't help wanting to level the playing field just a bit. She took in his baggy gray sweats with NYPD tattooed down the left side and his ragged T-shirt that revealed his abdomen. Never had she seen such a sexy man. A man so comfortable in his own skin and with his own masculinity.

God, she loved him. Letting him go might kill her, and though she'd give them her best shot, she'd also keep her promise and let him walk away if he chose. "You need to do something for me."

"I hardly think you're in the position to be asking for favors," he said with a grin.

She laughed. "Strip for me, Ben. Make us equal and then you can ravish me any which way you desire."

His eyes glazed over even more. "I hope you're not looking for music and dancing."

She shook her head. "All I need is you."

He drew a shuddering breath, reaching for the bottom of his shirt, then he whipped it over his head and tossed it onto the floor in one easy movement. His pants came off next, as he released the drawstring knot and pushed them down. They pooled around his ankles and he kicked them aside, leaving him standing nude.

Fully aroused and completely nude.

"No underwear?"

He shrugged. "Ran out. A certain someone's kept me too busy to even think about basic things like laundry."

She laughed, but she couldn't draw her gaze from his erection. Though they'd made love more than once, his sheer size and strength was almost more than she could handle. Her nipples puckered and dampness trickled between her legs. There was nothing she could do to hide her feminine reactions from him, even if she wanted to.

And she didn't want to because opening herself to him in every way imaginable was the only chance she had of keeping him by her side when this was over. She was completely exposed and his to take as he desired.

He eased himself beside her on the bed and placed a warm, comforting hand on her thigh. At least it was comforting until he rotated his wrist and eased his palm over her mound.

"So hot, so wet. For me," he murmured. He slid his fingers over her sensitive folds, arousing her full and wanting flesh.

With a sigh, she shut her eyes and gave herself up to sensation. To Ben. Grace refused to look, finding the sensations twice as erotic in the dark, with bound hands and legs open wide.

She felt the weight and dip of the mattress as he moved. Yet she was shocked when she felt his lips on her inner thigh, even more surprised when those same lips found her most feminine secrets and drank them in. His strong hands held her legs wide, locking them in place, while his mouth worked a magic she'd never felt before. His tongue traced her shape, learning her taste and discovering what made her moan, what made her writhe, what she liked best.

Grace learned that if she groaned a certain way, that wicked tongue would delve deeper, if her hips rose of their own volition off the mattress, his fingers would part her folds, giving him greater access to nip and graze with his teeth, then soothe with wide laps of his tongue. His touch was always gentle, and ever increasing in tempo and pressure. Her body quivered on the edge of release, yet not once did he take her over the edge.

He brought her so close. With caresses of his tongue against her swollen flesh, he took her higher. With a suckling, pulling maneuver, he sent her soaring, teetering at the brink. The waves would begin to build, only to retreat, climax always just out of reach.

And with each near-crescendo, the spiraling need grew higher, the pounding in her swollen flesh became harder and more insistent until her hands grabbed for the iron bars on the headboard and her hips shook hard and fast.

His technique was flawless. Not that of a man who knew women well, but that of the one man who took the time to learn *her* well.

Grace couldn't take another minute of his loving torture. She needed him to take the edge off, to let her climax and allow those rapturous waves to take over and buffet her body with painful yet exquisite force and completion.

He nibbled gently on that solitary spot he'd found, the one that let her crest the fastest, with the most teasing intensity.

"Oh, please!" The words ripped from the depths of her soul. "Please," she said on a sob, her eyes still closed, her hands still clenched and her body strung tight with wanting.

Without warning, he was on top of her, thrusting deep inside her, harder and faster than she'd ever experienced, filling the empty places and giving her exactly what she'd begged for. And everything about his rigid flesh felt magnified in intensity and beauty. Each long inch, each hard ridge of his erection eased her distress yet built it higher until without warning, he pulled back, leaving her bereft.

"Again." She hardly recognized the begging, pleading voice as her own. How could she when her sensitized, quivering body didn't feel familiar, either? She'd never *felt* so much before.

His glittering gaze met hers, revealing a depth and intensity of feeling that mirrored her own, causing a knot of emotion to well up inside her and threaten to burst.

Yet still he waited. For something, for what, Grace didn't know. "Ben!" She lifted her hips and called out his name.

Satisfaction filled his gaze and darkened his features as he grabbed for her shoulders and thrust deep. Then nothing could stop the climax that he'd forestalled for so long. As he moved inside her, gliding in and out, each motion making her feel more, want more, her orgasm burst inside her like an explosion, ripping away everything that was safe and leaving her raw and more exposed than ever.

But she wasn't alone and Ben was with her, holding her, cherishing her and coming at exactly the same moment with equal force. As the quivers lessened but didn't subside, he pulled her hair off her face and brushed her lips with his. Not a soft, gentle kiss, but a possessive, demanding one that brought tears back to her eyes.

He collapsed on top of her, spent as she was, but she welcomed the warmth, weight and feel of him against her.

And then he whispered in her ear. "Happy birthday, Gracie."

I love you, she thought, but kept the words locked in her heart, sensing he wouldn't want to hear.

BEN RELEASED THE MATERIAL shackling her arms and drew her close. He massaged first one delicate wrist, then the other, realizing for the first time the magnitude of trust she'd put in him when she allowed him to bind her arms and be at his mercy. Grace valued her independence and her freedom, yet she'd allowed him to restrain her—no questions asked.

"Are you okay?"

She curled into him. "Never better."

He relaxed with her under the covers, the scent of musky lovemaking and coconut oil filling the air around them, just as contentment filled him—so much it scared him.

He, a man who needed no one, needed this woman as much as he needed oxygen to breathe. Not an easy admission. And no easy solutions in sight.

Except the truth.

Something he wasn't ready to reveal. Not until he'd straightened out a few things first, and not on a birthday he'd promised himself Grace would never forget—for good reasons, not bad.

"Grace, we need to talk."

Her palm splayed on his stomach while her fingertips dipped lower. "Talking's overrated."

His erection twitched in agreement. He wanted her again. "Not when it comes to your safety. You took a risk today. A huge risk."

Her hand stilled. "I know. I didn't want to waste any time."

"I respect your independence but next time you pull a stunt like that I might have to resort to this." He waved the bandanna in the air.

"And that's supposed to deter me?" Her eyes glazed at the memory of being tied and at his mercy. She sighed. "But you're right. I took a huge risk. I'm sorry if I made you worry and I appreciate your coming after me."

"What, no anger?"

She shrugged. "I've done a lot of thinking lately. I've broken free from the family, the money and the strings attached. To do that, I needed to prove to myself I could be independent. I'm just sorry I scared you in the process."

"Well, I suppose I can forgive you." He kissed the top of her head.

"You're too generous." She laughed. "I guess that means I can admit that I don't mind you being my protector when it's warranted. You know, it actually feels good to know someone cares enough to want to take care of me. Better than someone doing it because my father paid them to."

He sucked in air but choked anyway. He hated living this lie. A few more loose ends and it was over. Too bad he had no idea how it would end.

He let out a deep breath and refocused on Grace. "You need to forget the Montgomery issues and put them behind you."

She curled into him and her warmth seeped inside him. "It's gotten easier with you around." She yawned and he leaned over to flick off the light.

Seconds passed in silence, turning into long minutes. Had he ever thought he'd find such peace with a woman by his side? And Grace Montgomery, of all women—a client's granddaughter, from a family so different from his own. He swallowed a laugh.

Though a part of him still believed Grace would miss the luxuries one day, he dismissed that part as prejudiced—as the part of him who'd disdained wealth as a kid. Not the man who knew Grace Montgomery and her goodness now.

No doubt about it, he'd fallen too hard to walk away. But if he chose to fight he had one hell of an uphill battle ahead of him.

GRACE AWOKE WITH A JOLT. She wasn't sure what had woken her, but once up, she tossed and turned, unable to fall back to sleep. She glanced over at the man sleeping by her side. His body heated her bed, just as he melted her heart. How had she gotten used to his presence so quickly? And how would she get used to being alone again once he was gone?

She flicked on a small lamp in the corner of the room. She wasn't surprised that Ben didn't stir. When the mighty P.I. crashed, ten thousand drummers couldn't wake him.

And she'd worn him out. She felt the corners of her mouth turn upward at the memory. His lips had touched places she'd considered private, branding her and marking her his own. And she'd let him. Because nothing had been more sacred than her heart, and he'd stolen that without even trying.

In sleep, his hair fell over his forehead, making him

lose some of the tough facade he exuded during the day. But none of the sexiness vanished. Sensuality was too much a part of him. He lay on his back, one arm over his head, the sheet dipping low at his waist. The dark hair on his chest trailed in an enticing line down his abdomen, disappearing beneath the covers. And what lay beneath...

She trembled at the memory. Her heart beat faster and moist arousal set her body throbbing. Grace didn't need to see what lay beneath the covers because she'd memorized him in intimate detail. Not only the sight of his erection, hard and ready just for her, but also the feel of him beneath her hand, and inside her body. For the first time she understood the mixed metaphor that described that body part, velvet and steel. His skin felt smooth to the touch, yet hard and strong with ridges able to arouse her in an instant.

If only it ended there. If only sex and desire were all she felt for Ben. Life would be so much easier. She eased herself beside him on the mattress. Buried deep inside the tough private investigator was a softness he let few people see. A childhood of hard work and deprivation had shaped him, but Grace had seen a more vulnerable side: his love for his ailing mother, dedication to the poorer kids of the world, and his concern for Grace and the lengths to which he would go to look out for her welfare. Beneath the tough guy exterior which drew her was the man Grace Montgomery loved.

Quietly she stood and crossed the room. She lifted her camera and raised it, focusing in on Ben. She'd snapped photos of him involved in various activities, but the man in her bed was the man of her dreams, and if she missed this opportunity she might never have another one. And Grace had a hunch these photos would be all she'd have to sustain her heart and soul in the lonely nights ahead.

Swallowing over the lump in her throat, she began to take pictures, walking around the room and capturing him from different angles. In her heart she knew these were the best pictures she'd ever taken. Because they held so much a part of her in each shot.

With each click of the shutter or flash of light, Grace cringed, not wanting him to wake up before she was through. But even if he rose now, she'd still have her treasured photos. And soon, that might be all she had left of Ben Callahan.

12

GIVING GRACE THE FREEDOM to go to work the next day and then to the park by herself was one of the hardest things Ben had ever done. Not because he worried about her safety, but because it represented the end.

The end of the case for Emma was a mixed blessing. By definition, he'd accomplished all the older woman had asked, and his job here was complete. He'd tried to call Emma all morning and into late afternoon to let her know, but according to the servants she wasn't available for phone calls. He didn't know what the hell that meant exactly, except he'd have to stall his final report—a report he no longer wanted to give.

He glanced at his watch. It was nearing five and he still had to bring the massage gear downstairs and leave it with the doorman, so he pulled the key Grace had given him out of his pocket and let himself inside her apartment.

As he walked through the living room and entered her bedroom, the scent of coconut oil assaulted his senses. The musky fragrance would never remind him of the beach again. Instead he'd forever associate the scent with Grace lying nude, arms loosely bound, eyes wide and hazy with desire, waiting for him to possess her. The trust she'd given him would be in his heart forever. He just hoped that once Grace found out the truth, he'd have a chance at forever.

He paused at the nightstand to collect the cassettes and bottles of oil when his gaze fell upon the bed. Grace had obviously been busy today, but not just at the photography studio where she worked. Now that he thought about it, they'd parted this morning and he'd only assumed she was going to the studio for the day. Apparently she'd had other things to do, including developing pictures.

Lying on the bed was an unopened album and photos were spread around the mattress. Photos of Ben. Of Ben unloading his Mustang, shooting hoops in the park, washing his car...and sleeping in her bed last night.

Shock held him still. For the first time in his career, he got a glimpse of what it felt like to be the subject and not the investigator. Of being observed without knowing it. He'd never considered his subjects feelings before, but now he had his own to contend with. He ought to feel violated, and would have if the person on the other side of the camera were anyone other than Grace.

He remembered the prickling feeling of being watched the day he washed his car and how quickly he'd shrugged off his unease. Some private investigator he was, Ben thought wryly. The P.I. had been set up, and a part of him admired Grace's ability to catch him unaware.

Easing himself onto the bed, he lifted the photos one at a time, examining them through a detached eye. As a photographer, Grace was good. He'd already seen her more precious photos and knew how well she captured life. She'd definitely do an incredible job on the CHANCES brochure and bring in substantial money for the charity. Everything stopped in that one second Grace caught on film, but the vivid, vibrant scenes were powerful and perfect.

As he pored over these shots, Ben realized she hadn't just taken pictures of him. She'd captured his soul. Every facet of his personality, from the bad-boy attempting to be one with the kids from the street, to the relaxed man hosing down his car on a Saturday morning, to the man sated by her lovemaking. She'd seen and savored them all.

He broke into a sweat, realizing just how well this woman knew him. She'd said her photos were a reflection of her feelings for the world around her and he had proof in his hands. Emotion showed in every picture, and as he saw himself through her eyes, he realized she was in deep.

As deep as Ben, and he was in love.

He muttered a curse. For as often as he'd contemplated his own feelings, he'd never factored in the possibility that Grace could fall in love with him. He'd been too absorbed by the impossibility of their situation and their extreme differences.

Differences that still existed.

His heart thundered loud in his chest and he realized that though he wanted a way out, finding one would hurt her badly. Love, caring—he felt them all for Grace, but would she forgive him for his deception? Would the woman seeking a life apart from the Montgomery family name understand that he'd kept one glaring truth from her—that he'd been hired by Emma Montgomery to keep tabs on her?

He placed the pictures back where he'd found them and rose. One last look at the bed where he'd spent the best moments of his life and Ben let himself out the door. He didn't want to be there when Grace came home because he needed time to think.

The truth, the one thing that could give them a future, could also tear them apart. But even if he wanted to come clean with Grace, professional ethics and his respect for Emma demanded he speak to the older woman first, before revealing both of their roles in the deception.

If Emma was angry, and she had every reason to be, she could demand he return the money he'd spent on the case—and Ben needed to factor his mother's situation and his finances into the equation before making any rash, selfish decisions. If it was just Ben, he was prepared to refund every penny he'd made on this case, but he was responsible for his mother, too.

But, he realized, his mother would understand. He could take that one burden off his shoulders. Having experienced love, she wouldn't deny her son the same thing, even if it meant delaying her move or sacrificing for him.

But Ben cared enough about his mother and Grace to find a way to make it work. He'd just find another way to pay for his mother's care, to take on more cases and be less discriminating about his clientele from now on. The chance to have Grace by his side was worth any sacrifice.

But there was the biggest risk of all—the one that scared him more than anything—and that risk was Grace. When disclosure was over, she could very well walk out on him anyway.

GRACE RACED OUT OF THE STUDIO. She wasn't sure why, but she had the strongest compulsion to get home—almost as if she feared Ben would be gone if she didn't rush fast enough. So she ran, promising herself that as soon as she saw him, as soon as she got her hands on him, she'd use that one word most men feared. The word *she* feared would send him away for good.

But Grace was through hiding. Before meeting Ben, she knew she wanted out of her shell, out of the protection and false sense of security the Montgomery name and money offered. She'd shed all of those trappings, but not until she'd gotten involved with Ben did she discover the essence of the woman she was.

Grace Montgomery wasn't impressed with status or money nor was she affected by appearances. She cared more for what existed in someone's heart than in their wallet, and found honesty more of a turn-on than pretense.

She found Ben so very attractive not because of his inherent sexiness, although she had to admit his appearance lured her in at first. But she gravitated toward Ben because he was the antithesis of everything she'd grown up with—because he was open and honest and real. Even when he was admitting his aversion to commitment, he was trusting her with the truth.

Before she let him go for good, she owed him the truth. She loved him and had every intention of telling him. Even if it drove him away forever.

She entered her apartment, surprised to find the door open. "Ben?" Though she'd left him her key to return Marcus's supplies, she couldn't imagine him being so careless as to leave her door unlocked. "Are you still here?"

"Still here? I just got here. It was the longest trip. Of course if I still had my license, I'd have made it doing eighty-five but your stick-in-the-mud father made sure I'll never get behind the wheel again. Imagine sitting in the back of a limousine for three hours while the driver does sixty."

"Gran?" Grace dropped her bag and ran for the living room.

"Who else has the key to your apartment?" Emma stood in the center of the room, arms open wide.

Grace met her halfway and found herself enveloped in her grandmother's thin arms. Thank goodness they still had a great deal of strength and as always they made her feel both safe and loved. "First Logan and Cat, now you. What are you doing here?"

"Like I'd let another birthday pass without a visit." Emma pushed Grace away and held her at arm's length for inspection. "You're beautiful. You could use a little meat on those bones, but you're still my Gracie."

A lump rose to her throat. It had been so long since her grandmother had resorted to her childhood name. Long enough that even Ben's use of the endearment hadn't evoked childhood memories, only adult yearning.

She took a moment to admire her grandmother in return. Although older with each visit, Emma was still regal and beautiful, her white hair pulled up in the same bun she'd always worn, and her designer suit was spotless and unwrinkled despite the long car ride to New York. "You look wonderful, Gran."

"Of course I do." The older woman grinned. "And thank goodness you have my genes. But you're avoiding the question, young lady. Who else has the key to your apartment?"

Grace took her grandmother's weathered hand and led her to the couch. "We have a lot to talk about." Suddenly the months of silence became a burden and Grace wanted to unload on the only person who would understand and accept.

Emma wouldn't judge because she'd raised Grace

to be her own person and make her own choices. But the first time Emma met Ben, Emma would pump him for so much information he'd think he was facing a CIA interrogation. Grace hoped she'd be able to either warn Ben or give her grandmother enough facts to forestall the inquisition.

"There's a man," Grace began, and decided to hold nothing back. "And I love him."

As if on cue, there was a knock on her door, followed by the sound of the key in the lock. *Ben.* His timing was awful. She'd had no time to prime Emma or to warn him about what was to come. Add to that, Emma's visit would prevent Grace from laying out her feelings to Ben.

Yet she couldn't regret the spontaneous visit. She'd missed her grandmother as much as she'd missed her brother. Sitting for hours on end couldn't be easy for Emma, not at her age, yet she'd made the trip anyway.

"I take it that's him now?" Emma asked.

"Yes, and behave yourself." Not that Grace believed her warning would do a bit of good. If Emma wanted to be precocious, nothing could stop her.

"I always do. Is this the neighbor your brother met?"

"Yes," Grace said quickly, before Emma could elaborate on what else Logan had seen. She only hoped her brother had been discreet.

"Grace?" Ben's voice carried into the apartment and his footsteps followed. "We need to talk."

"There seems to be a lot of that going around," Emma said with a laugh.

"Hush." Grace grit her teeth. Although she couldn't be happier to see her grandmother, Emma's nosiness was the one negative aspect of her surprise visit.

"I hope now's a good time..." His voice trailed off as he entered the living room, stopping short at the sight of Grace and her guest.

"Hi, Ben," Grace said.

He nodded at both women. Shock registered on his face.

She supposed he'd had his fill of surprise Montgomery visits in the past few days. "I'd like you to meet my grandmother." Grace rose, and helped Emma to her feet. "I've told you so much about her I'm sure you feel as if you know her already."

Ben's smile froze on his face.

Meeting the family, Grace thought. Ben couldn't possibly be happy about this turn of events. Still she was thrilled that the two people she loved most in the world could actually meet face-to-face.

She turned to Ben. "Ben, this is my grandmother, Emma Montgomery. Gran, this is my...new neighbor, Ben Callahan."

Since Ben's possession of her key made his relationship to Grace more than obvious, she opted just to call him a neighbor to spare him any further embarrassment. Emma would draw whatever conclusions she chose anyway, regardless of the words Grace used.

"A pleasure." Her grandmother beamed at Ben.

The sight of a man in Grace's apartment obviously did Emma's heart good. After Grace's dateless years and the lack of information Grace gave the older woman, her grandmother's teeth were probably chattering with excitement over the prospect of a live suitor to interrogate.

Emma extended her hand and he grasped it, shaking gently. "Same here."

Emma shook her head. "I'd expect a stronger grip from the man my granddaughter chose."

Grace was unable to stifle a laugh.

Ben colored and pumped Emma's hand with more gusto.

"That's better. Now sit and regale me with details. At my age I don't get near enough exposure to pheromones at work. The good Lord knows your parents sleeping in separate bedrooms hardly gets my blood pumping."

Grace rolled her eyes. Her parents had been in separate bedrooms for as long as she could remember—except when they were arguing. It wasn't a secret, but she didn't like her grandmother to reveal private family details or embarrass Ben with her penchant for sexual innuendo at the most inopportune moment. And based upon his uncharacteristic silence, Emma had not only embarrassed him, but she had him at a loss for words.

Grace sighed. If she wasn't careful, Emma would drive Ben away long before the words *I love you* even left Grace's mouth. "Behave yourself, Gran."

The older woman snorted. "Okay, then you two sit together and let me revel in young love."

"Mrs. Montgomery..."

"It's Emma," her grandmother said pointedly. "And I'm genuinely glad you're here. If my granddaughter likes you, that's good enough for me. Gracie, open a bottle of wine."

Grace narrowed her gaze. She'd expected Emma's approval, if only because her grandmother trusted Grace's judgment. But she'd also expected Emma to hit the man up with twenty questions, not accept him at face value.

And it bothered Grace beyond reason that Emma was so accepting. Not because she wanted to subject Ben to the Spanish Inquisition but because she didn't understand why her grandmother wasn't pushing harder. Grace's prom date had gotten a more difficult time, and he'd been nothing more than a close friend.

"Why don't you two get to know each other and I'll see if I can find a decent bottle of wine." Maybe if she left them alone, Emma would talk. And maybe then the uneasy feeling in the pit of Grace's stomach would disappear.

Emma nodded. "Good idea. Have a seat, Ben."

Grace let out a long stream of air. So there was hope for Emma yet.

Ben edged closer to Emma on the couch slowly, as

if facing a firing squad instead of her eighty-year-old spitfire of a grandmother. "Don't let her intimidate you, Ben," she called over her shoulder, then disappeared into the kitchen.

Grace knelt and began a search of the one cabinet that might have some wine or something Emma would enjoy drinking. Coming up empty, she rose and glanced through the pass-through. Emma and Ben sat together on the couch, deep in conversation.

Like two coconspirators.

The uneasy feeling returned. She rounded the corner and joined them in the living room. Silence surrounded them. A silence so unlike Emma that a proverbial tingle raced up Grace's spine.

"No wine," she said inanely.

Emma shrugged.

"I know you two must have a lot of catching up to do so..." Ben began to stand.

Grace stopped him with a hand on his shoulder. "Please, don't go."

He eased himself back into the seat beside Emma. "Your grandmother said she'd like to see my Mustang sometime."

"Oh, really."

"Yes. I adore old cars."

Grace narrowed her eyes. "Since when? You like new. Brand, spanking, sparkling new. The flashier the better, isn't that what you said when the judge refused to retire his old Lincoln Town Car? You talked about burying him in it," she muttered.

"Well, yes, but your father's a stick-in-the-mud. Ben here's old car would have character."

"You barely know Ben, so just how would you know that?" Grace placed her hands on her hips and faced her grandmother. "And you haven't asked him a single prying question since he walked in the door. That's unlike you, even with someone you know well. And you never met Ben before today so he's a prime candidate for your meddling..." Grace's voice trailed off.

She froze. Without warning, snatches of conversation came back to her. *My grandmother handpicked Cat. Set them up and locked them in a closet together. Her matchmaking shenanigans would put the most seasoned pro to shame...*

Impossible. Her grandmother and Ben had never met before today.

Emma patted Ben's hand. "Gut instinct, dear. He seems like a good boy and I trust your judgment. You know that."

Grace suddenly recalled with startling clarity Logan's wedding reception on the beach, along with Emma's teasing words: *Grace, you're my final project. I refuse to leave this earth without seeing you happily settled down. I think a trip to New York City is in order.*

She shook her head harder. Impossible, she thought again. Then why did the two of them look so guilty? "What are they hiding?"

"We're not hiding anything. I'm just pleased that everything worked out the way I'd hoped." Emma spoke at the same time Grace realized she'd asked the question aloud.

"And how's that?" Grace asked, still wary.

"You know me. I just want you settled and happy." Emma shifted in her seat, fidgeting uncomfortably.

"And what did you do to make that happen?" Grace glanced back and forth between Emma and Ben. "What could you possibly have done? Because it's obvious to me you're hiding something."

"Nonsense." But Emma didn't meet her gaze.

"Ben?" Grace captured his attention. "What is it my grandmother won't tell me?"

"Grace, can we talk about this later, when we're alone?"

Her mouth grew dry. "Up till now, I was working on a hunch. On gut instinct and no concrete evidence. But since you've just all but admitted there *is* something between you two, it's time you filled me in." She placed her hands on her hips. "Right now."

"I'd rather not do this now." Ben's reluctance couldn't be more obvious.

Emma placed a hand on his arm and Grace knew something was wrong. "I think she's got us cornered," Emma said, looking none too happy at the prospect.

The uneasiness in Grace's stomach turned into painful cramping. "Cornered about what?" she asked though she already knew—or thought she did.

"This damn charade," Ben said. He walked closer to Grace and tried to touch her cheek.

She stepped back, needing the space to think. "So you know each other."

"We've met," Emma hedged.

Graced folded her arms across her chest. "Deliberately vague doesn't cut it, Gran. Met how? Where?"

Ben and Emma met each other's gaze, each it seemed, imploring the other to fill Grace in on their secret. As she waited, her heart pounded harder in her chest.

Finally Ben spoke first. "We met at the Montgomery Estate a few weeks back, when Emma hired me." He let out a groan, running a hand through his already disheveled hair.

"Hired you?" This was a scenario she'd never envisioned.

He shook his head. "We can talk about this later. Please."

She heard the plea in his voice and ignored it. "Hired you to do what?" she asked again.

"To keep tabs on you and fill her in on your activities." The words seemed to be drawn from inside him painfully, but the knowledge that he hurt, too, didn't soften the blow.

"But you have to understand Emma's reasons," he went on. "You were keeping her in the dark and she was concerned."

"It's kind of you to stick up for my grandmother's meddling, but it doesn't exonerate her. Or you. It's too little information and too late for the reasons to matter." Grace lowered herself into the nearest chair, agony tearing her apart.

The man she'd thought had nothing to do with the Montgomery family name or money had been paid for all the attention he'd shown her. He hadn't learned about her life or looked out for her welfare because he cared. He hadn't fallen for *just Grace* at all.

The sense of betrayal rose, clogging her throat with a lump so big she couldn't swallow. She could barely speak. No wonder he couldn't promise anything beyond their short time together—when Emma was no longer laying out cash for his services, Ben intended to be gone.

Grace looked up, not surprised to see her grandmother couldn't meet her gaze. But Ben's eyes bore into hers. She'd seen those eyes glazed by passion and lightened by laughter. Now emotion flickered in the darkened depths and she wanted to grasp onto those emotions like a lifeline.

How pathetic, Grace thought. Because she wanted some ray of hope, she was willing to see caring where there was none. She'd only thought she'd caught glimpses of his innermost thoughts and feelings, only deluded herself into thinking he was falling as hard for her as she'd fallen for him.

She'd believed it because she believed she knew him. But looking at Ben now, the lies and deception exposed, she didn't know him at all. And it hurt. Badly.

"Grace..." His voice intruded on her pain.

She shook her head. She didn't want to hear anything he had to say. What could possibly excuse such a colossal lie? Just doing his job would only have held water until their relationship turned from neighbors to lovers. At that point he might not have desired forever, but he could have told her the truth.

"If you'll just let me explain." Emma sounded more fragile than usual and Grace understood. She felt as if she, herself, might shatter if she had to hear any more.

She needed to get away from them. From the two people she loved most, and the two who had betrayed her.

13

GRACE SLAMMED THE APARTMENT door shut behind her. Ben didn't try to stop her. The shattered look of hurt that had flashed across her delicate features would live inside him forever. If getting away from them helped, he was all for letting her go.

He turned to Emma. The older woman lowered herself into a seat, looking weary. "There had to be a better way to tell her."

He wasn't sure if she'd have taken the news any better coming from him first and him alone, but he'd never know. Emma's arrival had destroyed any hope of letting Grace down gently.

"I had the best of intentions but I still hurt her badly."

Ben placed a hand on Emma's shoulder. "It wasn't your fault." If he'd kept his hands to himself, if he'd done his job and gotten out, if he'd remained detached and uninvolved, none of this would ever have happened.

Of course he'd have missed out on the best thing to come along in his lifetime, but he wasn't the person who counted. That was Grace.

"Sit down, Benjamin."

He blinked, certain he hadn't heard Emma correctly. No one called him Benjamin, not even his mother, and Emma couldn't possibly have regained her spunk and fortitude so quickly. One glance into those regal brown eyes and he realized he'd underestimated her again.

So Ben did the only thing he could under the circumstances. He sat.

"I won't have you blaming yourself for my meddling. Make no mistake. I'd heard wonderful things about you professionally and I needed your assistance to keep an eye on my granddaughter, but I took one look at you and I just knew you'd be good for Grace. Women's intuition, you understand." Emma tapped at her head and nodded.

Ben didn't understand. "You're telling me you hired me for a legitimate business reason but you wanted me to get involved with your granddaughter?"

Emma nodded.

So he'd been set up as much as Grace. Somehow Ben doubted the knowledge would make her feel any better. And considering he'd had a choice every step of the way, he was still disgusted with his actions and the hurt they'd caused.

He clenched his hands into fists at his side and faced Grace's grandmother. "I don't like being played for a fool."

"I saw the look on your face the minute you laid eyes on her picture. And can you deny the chemistry between you two now? Can you deny you've fallen in love with her?"

Ben's stomach clenched hard. Thinking it to himself and hearing the words aloud were very different things. Yet faced with Grace's beloved grandmother, he couldn't lie. Not even in the wake of the older woman's meddling ways. Not even when he was dealing with the very real possibility that he'd lost Grace for good.

"I'm not sure how I feel matters anymore. She's not likely to forgive the lies and, frankly, I wouldn't blame her." He gazed around the expensively decorated apartment, seeing how even this environment was a facet of Grace, one he loved as much as the fun-loving, down-to-earth woman who lived here.

Without warning, Emma smacked him hard on the shoulder. He glanced up, shocked at the strength in her frail bones and surprised she felt comfortable enough to whack him like that. "What was that for?"

"You're too much like Logan for your own good. Don't take things sitting down. You need to fight for what you want. If you're out of ideas I can help..."

"No, thank you." The older woman had done enough. "I can handle things on my own."

He doubted he could change the outcome but he could most definitely have his one-on-one with Grace before she threw him out of her life. At the very least she deserved to understand what motivated his actions, even if the explanation couldn't make up for the pain of his deception.

Ben stood. "Can I get you anything before I go?"

Emma glanced up at him, concern and caring in her eyes. "You can tell me my granddaughter's okay."

He grasped her hand and held on tight. "She's fine. Or at least she was fine until tonight." Time to lay all his cards on the table, Ben thought. "There won't be any further report, written or otherwise."

Emma nodded in understanding. "I'm past wanting details anyway. I see now how wrong that really was."

"Good because I can't give you any more information about Grace and still live with myself. But I can refund what money you've laid out for this assignment, and if I run short, I swear to you I'll pay you back in installments."

The older woman clucked her tongue in a gesture reminiscent of his mother. "Nonsense. You did your job and I pay for services rendered."

And that, Ben thought, was the ultimate problem. If he accepted any of Emma's money, Grace would never believe his interest in her was real, separate and apart from the Montgomery name and Montgomery money. Even if he didn't, she might not believe him.

Because Ben had made her biggest fear come true and had probably decimated the self-worth she'd worked so hard to achieve. He'd recently been so sure that she would return to her privileged lifestyle once the novelty of independence wore off. But now he knew she would never abandon a life that had been so right for her. A life he'd now undercut with his deceit.

He didn't like himself much right now. "It's useless to argue about payment."

Emma nodded. "I agree. Your time would be better spent finding Grace, and since that's where you'd rather be, then I suggest you get to it."

"Tell me one thing first."

"What's that?"

"Why are you so accepting of someone you know doesn't have your family background or status? Someone who'll make Grace's judge father cringe at best?" He voiced the question that had been nagging at him.

Emma treated him to a genuine smile. "That's simple. You make my granddaughter happy."

Maybe he had once. But not anymore.

Yet he found it impossible to dislike or remain angry with Emma Montgomery, no matter how much trouble she caused or how irrepressible she chose to be. Deep down she had a heart of gold.

Like Grace.

Ben had broken that heart. He only hoped he could undo some of the damage he'd caused. If not, he'd live with the consequences—and emptiness—for the rest of his life.

BEN APPROACHED HER FROM behind. He'd found her at the park, kicking at the sand in the sandbox. She could have been a kid who'd lost her best friend, but

Ben knew better. She was a woman who'd lost her lover and her faith in a man she'd trusted. The anguish couldn't be smoothed over with a stick of candy or a kiss on the cheek. Much as he'd like to try.

He came up beside her and eased himself onto the wooden planks surrounding the sand. "Hi, there."

She didn't glance up. "I suppose that's just one of the drawbacks of you being a private investigator. The ability to find people who don't want to be found."

"If you didn't want to be found you wouldn't have come here." Ben drew a deep breath. "I didn't find you because of professional skills. I found you because I know *you*."

"Too bad I can't say the same." She laughed, but it wasn't the lighthearted laugh he'd come to associate with Grace and his gut twisted with the knowledge that he'd taken that away from her.

All he could do was explain. "When I took the case I didn't know you. Working for Emma was just another assignment."

"That paid extremely well, no doubt."

He wished he could deny it. "Would it make a difference if I said I needed the money to get my mother into assisted care?"

She kicked at the dirt once more. "I'm not angry with you for taking a job. You're entitled. I just can't understand how you could...sleep with me knowing you were taking money to get close to me. I don't understand how you...how we did the things we did together and you never once tried to tell me the truth."

She swiped at a tear dripping down her face and his gut clenched with regret and shame. Mere words wouldn't undo the damage he'd caused.

Her brown eyes, absent of the light and life he adored, met his gaze. "And most of all I don't understand how you let me go on believing that what we shared was the one thing in my life separate and apart from my family's name and money."

Her voice cracked but she didn't quit talking and Ben didn't try to stop her.

"You knew how important my independence was. You knew, even if I never said it aloud, that my whole self-perception had been shaped by what my family could buy for me. But you—I never thought you could be bought. Not for me, not for anyone. Yet it turns out that's exactly what happened. Emma bought you. For me."

"Grace..."

She shook her head. "She bought your services as a private investigator as a ruse for you to get close to me. She hoped you'd fall in love with me. Because she didn't think I was worthy on my own."

Hearing her view of their situation, Ben thought he'd be sick. Not once had he believed he'd been bought to fall in love with Grace.

He'd done that all on his own. "Is it my turn yet?"

"Go ahead. But like I said earlier, it's too little, too late."

"Maybe so, but I'm not leaving until you hear me out."

Her arm swept the expanse of the park. "Free speech," she muttered. "I can't deny you that."

"Gee, thanks," he said wryly. "This is more serious than that."

She tipped her head to the side and looked at him through huge brown eyes. "More serious than constitutional rights? Then I suppose it needs to be said."

He grabbed for her ice-cold hand. "I'm not sure this is going to come out right. It's twisted in here." He pointed to his head. "And here." He tapped at his heart. "So I'm not positive I can even explain myself well to you. But I'll give it a shot."

Dusk was setting around them, the sun dipping below the buildings and a cool breeze chilled the air. But Ben wasn't going anywhere and, so far, neither was Grace.

This was his last opportunity. His last chance to win—or lose—the woman he loved. Considering she seemed to have her mind set against him, he doubted anything he said now would make a difference. But he couldn't live the rest of his life without trying.

"It was never just a job. From the second I saw your picture..."

"You saw my picture?" She shook her head. "Never mind. Emma's been foisting my photo on eligible males for as long as I can remember. Go on."

"From the minute I saw your picture, I was invested. I warned myself to back off, to let the case go, but I couldn't."

"The money."

"My mother, the money and you. All three got tangled together. She needs more care than I can provide right now. It'll take six months to a year of cases I wouldn't normally touch to make a large enough cushion to set her up in the home of her choice."

Unexpectedly Grace placed a hand on his arm. A heated tingling set up residence on his skin. "You love her. I can understand that."

"I'm not sure you can. You grew up in that mansion. I grew up on the other side looking in. I understand now that even without money I got the better end of the deal—because I had love and you didn't." He covered her hand with his.

"You had to perform for your father and still didn't get the love that should have been unconditional, the love you deserved. But, you had money. And servants." He let out a groan. "And my mother was one of them. Can you imagine what that's like? A woman who spent her life as a mother—a stay-at-home mother, suddenly finds herself a widow with little money. So she turns to the only thing she knows— housekeeping for others. And those others weren't as kind to the help as I suspect Emma is."

Grace shuddered, recalling her father's bellowing at the servants, as he called them, belittling them for little things not done correctly.

"And I knew how badly she was being treated and

that she put up with it to support me, us. But I couldn't do a damn thing about it until years later."

Grace watched Ben's face contort with remembered pain and she felt not only for him, but for his mother, a woman she'd never met. She understood his frustration at his youth and inability to do anything but watch his mother suffer to make his life better. She understood, too, that everything he did now was to compensate and make up for things he hadn't been able to change back then.

But that was the past while Grace was the present. And she'd been the one to pay for Ben's atonement. "I understand why you took the case. I don't understand why the minute our relationship became intimate you didn't come clean."

He ran a hand through his hair. "That's where things got tangled. I'd promised Emma secrecy. By virtue of taking the case, my professional ethics had to come first. And I know how lame it sounds now, but it's the truth."

She listened in silence so he kept going.

"There was also the attack and the threat. If I'd told you that I was working for Emma, you'd have kicked me out of your life. No way would you have let me close enough to make sure you were safe. I couldn't take the risk with your life."

"Because Emma was paying you to keep me safe."

"No! Because I cared too much to let you walk the streets alone and unprotected." His dark eyes held her captive and begged for her to believe.

She stared back, unwilling to be the one to break eye contact, wishing he'd pull her into his arms and knowing she'd break away if he did. As much as she wanted to believe him, she couldn't get past the fact that he'd been paid for every bit of interest he'd shown in her life. Taken to the extreme, he'd been paid by a family member she loved to sleep with her. And it hurt.

"So let me get this straight. You didn't tell me because you owed Emma your loyalty, and because you wanted to protect me from a threat on the street."

"That's right."

She kicked at the sand in the box hard, not caring that it sifted onto Ben. What was a little more dirt on his hands? "No, it's wrong. Because, let's face it, you took money from my grandmother and you felt a responsibility toward her. You took the money for your mother, to whom you also feel responsible. You, your mother and my grandmother. Every person in this scenario taken care of...except me."

She hated the self-pity in her voice, when it was the last thing she was feeling. Much stronger were anger and betrayal, hurt and pain for a love gone bad. One that obviously never existed. Not on his side anyway.

At least she could give him credit for not lying about feelings that didn't exist.

Hurt and disbelief flashed across his handsome face. "It wasn't like that." He stood and shoved his hands into his back pockets. "Summed up badly, I made a bad decision in the name of ethics, Gracie."

"I respect your ethics. I don't respect the lies."

"And I don't respect the fact that I couldn't keep my damn hands off you." He reached for her, grabbing her shoulders and pulling her close. "I still can't."

"I'm not sure if that's a compliment or not."

His hands traveled down her arms and up again. His body heat was potent, as was his sexuality and the love she still felt regardless that her feelings went unreciprocated.

"Trust me, it is." Ben groaned in frustration. "And if you believe nothing else, believe this: This mess didn't have anything to do with you. It had to do with me. I should have backed off. I should have kept things platonic. I shouldn't have gotten involved with a client's granddaughter, the subject of my investigation."

"Well, you did." The anger she'd been withholding resurfaced and she shoved him away. "You damn well did. Not only did you put your hands on me, but inside me, dammit. I was a woman you couldn't keep your hands off of, but not one you respected enough to tell the truth."

He sighed and stepped back, finally accepting the barriers she'd placed between them. "I understand you're hurt, Grace, but hurt doesn't change the feelings you had before you found out the truth."

She lifted her chin a notch. "And what would those be?"

"You love me."

Feeling as if she'd been punched in the stomach, she nearly doubled over. She held herself around the waist—anything to hold herself together until he was gone. "That's an arrogant assumption."

He shook his head. "It's fact. I saw the photos you took of me. No one's ever gotten that close. That deep. No one's cared enough to bother. So you can be hurt and betrayed. I wouldn't presume to take that away from you. But when the pain wears off, what'll happen to the love?"

She opened her mouth, then closed it again.

A tired smile pulled at his lips. "What's the matter? Cat got your tongue?"

She shook her head. "Unlike you, I can't bring myself to lie."

"That's good. Because it's just one of the things I love about you." He raised his hand in a wave, turned and respected her silent request. He left her alone, the way she'd been before he barged into her solitary existence.

The way she'd be for the rest of her life.

BEN LOADED THE LAST OF HIS things into the trunk of the Mustang. Moving out of the Murray Hill apartment and back into his studio in the Village should have made him happy. He'd never been comfortable in the yuppie apartment owned by the landlord's brother. Too little comfort for his taste. But having Grace across the hall had been worth the sacrifice.

In fact, having her in his life, even for a short time,

was a selfish blessing for a guy who didn't deserve one. If he'd been up-front with her sooner, maybe he'd be moving *in* with her instead of away. Then again if he'd told her he loved her as he'd wanted to last night, he might have eaten a mouthful of sand for dinner.

Ben had to face that a future with Grace was never meant to be. From the day he'd accepted Emma's money in exchange for keeping tabs on her grand-daughter, he'd sealed the impossibility of any long-term relationship. Coming clean sooner rather than later wouldn't have changed her feelings of betrayal. In her eyes, he'd used her and had been paid for the opportunity.

That was why he hadn't bothered telling her he had no intention of keeping Emma's money nor taking any further payment. It was also why he hadn't told her he loved her, too. From the bleak look in her eyes, it wouldn't have made a damn bit of difference.

He muttered a curse and slammed the trunk closed. As he turned, an uneasy feeling of being watched stole over him. Recalling the last time he'd had such a sensation and the resulting photos he'd seen in Grace's apartment, Ben had to laugh aloud.

Grace couldn't stand the sight of him. There was no chance in hell she cared enough to watch him out her window now. Unless she was waving goodbye.

GRACE LOWERED THE CAMERA and set it down on the dresser. Taking pictures of Ben as he loaded the trunk of his car and prepared to drive off was torture. Why she thought she'd find closure and peace in the act, she'd never know.

Instead she found herself standing by the window with tears pouring out of her eyes as she called herself a coward for refusing to confront Ben one more time.

"All you have to do is run downstairs and stop him."

Grace folded her arms across her chest and turned to face her grandmother. Because of Emma's age, apology and undying love for her granddaughter, Grace had forgiven her last night. If she hadn't kept Emma in the dark and caused her to worry, her grandmother wouldn't have hired a private investigator. Grace accepted that she'd taken her bid for independence too far. She'd been the one to set the chain of events in motion that led to this moment.

She glanced out the window once more. Ben stood talking to the doorman. One hip propped against the Mustang, his shirt hem ragged from being ripped at the seam and his sleeves cut by hand, he looked like the bad boy she'd fallen in love with.

"It's not the lie that's stopping you from going after him, is it?" Emma asked. "Because Lord knows you and Logan told me your fair share growing up and I'm still speaking to you both. Never took you across my knee, either." A wicked gleam sparked in Emma's gaze. "But that just might be a good punishment for your Ben."

Grace couldn't help but laugh despite the pain. "Cut it out, Gran. It's not the lie that's holding me back."

She'd gotten past that last night. Lying alone in the dark, remembering the time she and Ben had spent together, recalling the feel of his arms around her, Grace knew in her heart he was still the decent, honest man she'd pegged him to be. A man with too many responsibilities and too many people to answer to.

Emma had put him in an untenable position—she'd done it to Logan and Catherine before him. But Emma hadn't realized Ben had an ailing mother to consider on top of his own feelings. In the light of day, Grace could even respect his decision to remain silent in order to secure his mother's health and well-being.

She also recalled the intimacy they'd shared, and while she'd given him her body, she'd also given him her heart. He just hadn't felt the same. "He doesn't love me, Gran. He had fun with me. He cares about me. But he doesn't love me."

"And how do you know this? What makes you so certain?"

Grace swallowed over the lump in her throat. "Because he knows I love him, and he didn't say it back."

But she hadn't actually said it to him, either, Grace realized. Her heart began to pound hard in her chest.

Emma raised an eyebrow, a gesture Grace had become familiar with over the years. One that meant her grandmother had all the answers, while Grace or Logan or whoever she was lecturing had none.

"Since when do men lay their feelings on the line with words?" Emma asked.

Grace blinked. "Go on." She glanced out the window again. Ben still stood engrossed in conversation. She hadn't lost him—yet. And even without hearing what else Emma had to say, she already had one foot out the door—because she hadn't laid her feelings on the line, either, and suddenly she knew why.

She was a coward. She could let Ben go now and blame him for his lies, or she could accept his explanation and move on. Before Emma's shenanigans had blown up in her face, Grace had promised herself she'd tell Ben she loved him. If he'd still chosen to leave, she'd have stepped aside without another word, because he'd said no commitment and she'd given her promise that she'd let him go. But she'd never gotten the chance...because he'd never had the opportunity to reject her.

"Not everyone's as open with their feelings as I am," her grandmother said.

Grace laughed. "That's an understatement."

"And not everyone's as cold and unfeeling as your father. He may never have said he loved you, but he does in his own arrogant, I-want-her-to-fit-the-mold way. Doesn't excuse him for acting like an ass, but he loves you. And if you confronted him, he might just say it back. Or maybe he wouldn't, and you'd be left out there raw and exposed. Same way you've been for most of your life."

Grace blinked back tears. Her grandmother had just summed up her biggest fear—that Ben would reject her the same way her parents had. So instead of getting past the lie, she'd let it come between them. Because it was easier to blame Ben than set herself up for potential rejection.

But thanks to Ben she'd discovered the woman named Grace Montgomery. She learned she had an innate sensuality, a deep ability to love, and a heart-felt sense of honesty. How could she demand the truth from Ben if she wasn't willing to give it herself? And besides, hadn't she decided long before Ben that she was through hiding from life?

"The opposite sex is notorious for withholding their feelings. They won't chance putting themselves out there to be hurt. It's up to us women to make the first move. Where would we be if Eve hadn't eaten the apple? We certainly wouldn't be having all this fun, now would we?" Emma winked at Grace. "Well, what are you waiting for?"

Grace hugged her grandmother tight. "I've got to go."

"It's about time," Emma muttered.

As Grace ran for the door, her grandmother's voice followed after her. "Did I mention he's refusing to take my money?"

Grace laughed, feeling more hopeful than she had seconds earlier, and slipped into the hall.

BEN TOOK ONE LAST LOOK at the high-rise building and turned to get into his car. No point in indulging in lingering regrets or what-ifs, he thought. The end had come.

"Going somewhere?"

At the sound of Grace's soft voice, he turned fast. She faced him wearing a pair of denim shorts and a T-shirt. But she'd tucked the hem of the shirt between her breasts as she'd done the other day, exposing the pale skin on her stomach and accentuating her curves. His mouth grew dry just looking at her and his jeans grew too tight.

"I asked if you're going somewhere." She folded her arms across her chest.

He wasn't sure if she meant to be provocative, but the effect of her action pushed the rounded flesh up enticingly. "I was heading home."

She nodded. "You never did mention where home was."

"The Village." He had no desire to stand in broad daylight and converse with her like total strangers. Just being around Grace and not being able to touch her reminded him of his bad judgment and mistakes, of all the might-have-beens and things they'd never share.

He turned toward the car, away from her, away from the memories.

Her sudden hold on his wrist surprised him. "Running again?"

He recognized the challenge in her voice and took

heart. If she was stopping him from leaving, she had something to say. And he intended to stick around and hear every word.

The usual stream of people entered and exited the building. "How about we take this somewhere private?" He was deliberately teasing her, reminding her of the games they'd played, hoping she'd recall where those dares and challenges had ended up.

She grinned. "Sure thing." She swung around and her ponytail whipped behind her in a sassy move that turned him on even more. Now this was the Grace he liked to see—happy, playful, hopeful.

She grabbed for the handle of the car and opened the door, then pushed the driver's seat forward and slid into the back.

He met her gaze and grinned before hopping into the front seat, turning on the ignition and driving the car around to the side street behind the building where they'd parked once before. Faster than he thought possible, he turned off the ignition and maneuvered himself into the back seat along with her.

"Maybe I was wrong. Maybe you aren't running again after all." Her eyes glittered with hope and a touch of uncertainty. The uncertainty got to him, wrapping around his heart and not letting go.

He placed his knuckles beneath her chin and lifted her face to meet his gaze. "No more games, Gracie. I'm here and I'm not going anywhere. Not till you have your say and maybe not even after that."

She nodded. "I see that." Her voice trembled slightly.

Wanting to ease that vulnerability once and for all, he leaned within kissing distance. "You've got me alone, princess." Her darkened eyes met his. "Now what are you going to do with me?" Ben's pulse thudded so loud he would swear Grace could hear it, too.

"Did you mean it when you said you don't do commitment?"

Her question took him by surprise. "I meant it at the time. I didn't know I'd..."

"Didn't know you'd what? Because I love you, Ben, and it's a rough emotion to be feeling alone." Her brown eyes widened and she sat so still he was afraid she'd shatter if he botched his answer.

He hadn't realized how badly he needed to hear her say the words. Now that she had, his world righted itself once more. His heart kicked into high gear. "I didn't know I'd fall in love with you, too." He shook his head. "Yes, I did. In my gut I knew from the moment I laid eyes on that picture. But I couldn't let myself feel it any more than I could have told you the truth. But I should have. Because from the beginning you were more important to me than the case, than Emma, even more than my mother. And that's saying a lot."

She brushed her lips over his. Featherlight, the comforting kiss was still enough to tease and arouse, and make him want much more. "Speaking of your mother, you're taking Emma's money. And don't fight me on this if you ever want to get lucky again. And second, when do I get to meet her?"

Grace held her breath and waited. No more hiding. She'd conquered her fear but she still didn't know if she'd walk away with her heart intact. She hoped, but she needed proof.

She got it when Ben lifted her around the waist and pulled her onto his lap. She shifted until her legs straddled his thighs and she was back where she belonged. His erection pulsed hard and strong between her legs in a steady beat that echoed the need inside of her.

"We have a few things to take care of first."

"I take it you're not going anywhere?" she asked.

"Sweetheart, nothing and no one could tear me away from you. Not now, not ever."

He leaned forward and licked a tear off her cheek.

"You make me happy," she said.

"You always cry when you're happy?"

Grace laughed. "Stick around and find out."

_____Epilogue_____

EMMA HAD PEERED OUT the window, watching as Grace lured Ben into his car and together they disappeared around the corner. Then she'd let out a long sigh of relief.

This matchmaking business was draining for a woman of her age, she thought now as she lowered herself into a seat on the couch. If only young people today weren't so difficult her job would be so much easier.

But she'd accomplished her goals and with great success. Logan was happily married and Grace was well on her way. She patted her bun with satisfaction. If Ben was as good as Emma thought he'd be, he and Grace wouldn't return from around the corner for quite awhile. Thinking back to her youth, she knew that with a little imagination, a car could be a very inventive place for intimate relations.

She stretched her legs in front of her. They ached from yesterday's long car ride, but she'd never felt so happy or rejuvenated. Her presence was just what those two young kids needed to push them toward that final step—admitting their true feelings.

With Grace and Logan settled, Emma could rest

easy that her beloved immediate family was taken care of. But she couldn't sit still for long. No, a woman of her talent...it would be a shame to waste a precious minute of the time she had left on this earth.

And Emma planned to be around for a long time. Long enough to bounce Grace and Ben's children on her knee. But what would keep her occupied in the meantime?

Continue what she was good at! She snapped her fingers as the thought came to her. She had nieces and nephews that would be at her disposal in just a few years. In the meantime, her social set was full of widows, widowers and divorcées. All people in desperate need of companionship—even if they didn't know it yet. Most of them had had miserable first marriages, but they hadn't had Emma Montgomery to choose their mates.

She picked up the phone and dialed, pleased when Alice Farnsworth answered on the first ring. "Alice, I'm visiting my granddaughter but I'll be home tomorrow in time for the charity benefit at Wild Acres Country Club. My chauffeur's ill and I was wondering if you could pick me up."

She listened to her response. "No problem? Well, thank you. Did I mention I promised to drive poor Ralph Nadelson? He hasn't been the same since his wife passed on..."

Yes, Emma thought. She was born to matchmake, those little snafus not withstanding. She glanced at her watch. After all, Ben and Grace still hadn't resurfaced and it had been a good half hour or more.

Ah, to be young, and be able to make love all you wanted, 24/7. Grace and Ben were lucky, indeed.

Pamela Burford presents

The Wedding Ring

*Four high school friends and a pact—
every girl gets her ideal mate by thirty or be
prepared for matchmaking! The rules are
simple. Give your "chosen" man three
months...and see what happens!*

Love's Funny That Way
Temptation #812—on sale December 2000
It's no joke when Raven Muldoon falls in love with comedy
club owner Hunter—*brother* of her "intended."

I Do, But Here's the Catch
Temptation #816—on sale January 2001
Charli Ross is more than willing to give up her status as
last of a dying breed—the thirty-year-old virgin—to Grant.
But all *he* wants is marriage.

One Eager Bride To Go
Temptation #820—on sale February 2001
Sunny Bleecker is still waiting tables at Wafflemania when
Kirk comes home from California and wants to marry her.
It's as if all her dreams have finally come true—except...

Fiancé for Hire
Temptation #824—on sale March 2001
No way is Amanda Coppersmith going to let
The Wedding Ring rope her into marriage. But no matter
how clever she is, Nick is one step ahead of her...

**"Pamela Burford creates the
memorable characters readers love!"
—*The Literary Times***

It's hot...and it's out of control.

BLAZE

This winter is going to be ***hot, hot, hot!***
Don't miss these bold, provocative,
ultra-sexy books!

SEDUCED by Janelle Denison
December 2000

Lawyer Ryan Matthews wanted sexy Jessica Newman the
moment he saw her. And she seemed to want him, too, but
something was holding her back. So Ryan decides it's time
to launch a sensual assault. He *is* going to have Jessica in
his bed—and he isn't above tempting her with her own
forbidden fantasies to do it....

SIMPLY SENSUAL by Carly Phillips
January 2001

When P.I. Ben Callahan agrees to take the job of watching
over spoiled heiress Grace Montgomery, he figures it's easy
money. That is, until he discovers gorgeous Grace has a
reckless streak a mile wide and is a serious threat to his
libido—and his heart. Ben isn't worried about keeping
Grace safe. But can he protect her from his loving lies?

Don't miss this daring duo!

HARLEQUIN®
Temptation.

Tyler Brides

It happened one weekend...

Quinn and Molly Spencer are delighted to accept three bookings for their newly opened B&B, Breakfast Inn Bed, located in America's favorite hometown, Tyler, Wisconsin.

But Gina Santori is anything but thrilled to discover her best friend has tricked her into sharing a room with the man who broke her heart eight years ago....

And Delia Mayhew can hardly believe that she's gotten herself locked in the Breakfast Inn Bed basement with the sexiest man in America.

Then there's Rebecca Salter. She's turned up at the Inn in her wedding gown. Minus her groom.

Come home to Tyler for three delightful novellas by three of your favorite authors: Kristine Rolofson, Heather MacAllister and Jacqueline Diamond.

HARLEQUIN®
Makes any time special ™

Visit us at www.eHarlequin.com

PHTB